MW00454454

A WITCH,

IN TIME,

SAVES...

F. J. SCONZO, SR. & SPIRIT RISING

i

I want to thank my wife Evelynn for allowing me to spend the time in my imagination to write this story. Her love and support helped me get through many a dark passage.

I also would like to thank my co-writer and friend,

Spirit Rising, who helped immensely during the creation process; to entrap ideas from the minds, rip feelings from our souls to place upon these pages. Thanks for letting me rant and rave.

Also a thanks to our wonderful editor

E. V. FITZ for all her help with grammar and punctuation. I would have been lost.

A thank you to our IT Guy Frank, for the advice and help with the cover. "Thanks, Son!"

A big thank you to The Great Anne McCaffrey (1926-2011), my favorite writer, for showing me how to imagine.

And Breta Allan, my high school English teacher who showed me that it is always okay to dream. (Even in English class, sometimes.)

SOMEWHEN'- (sum~wen') adv.

A place in time when the planets align. The stars twinkle their brightest. The moon glow pervades upon the spirit causing a temporal rift in reality;

WHERE ANYTHING CAN HAPPEN

THE PAST CAN BE RE-LIVED ~

THE PRESENT IS SUSPENDED ~

AND THE FUTURE

IS A GIFT FROM THE GODS

PROLOGUE – CHINA circa 500 AD

The Samurai held tight the little girl's arm in a cruel grip. Crying, she reached for the blood splattered shawl held up for the Magistrate to see.

Two other guards held her parents.

"Do you know what your daughter did?"

The parents were horror-struck that this most important man would talk to them. It only meant more suffering and hardships.

The father screamed as the guard twisted his arm higher up his back in the submission hold.

"Answer The Magistrate," the guard hissed.

"No, Your Worship, I do not know," he whimpered.

"This shawl belongs to your child, does it not?" The man spat once, as if merely speaking to these lowlifes would foul his mouth.

Her father looked forlornly at his small, fragile Lian, thinking how great it would have been had she been a son. Then nodded his head in acceptance, knowing he could not deny her, or what was about to come.

The Magistrate pronounced, "The shawl was found by the sleeping mat of your over-seer. His throat was sliced. Since this shawl was found next to his body and it belongs to your daughter, I charge her with his murder."

Her mother wept uncontrollably.

"Lian was with us all day. The shawl was stolen last night while we slept."

The father begged forgiveness for his wife's outspokenness as the Samurai beat him into silence.

The trial over, the little girl, now alone in her prison cried hopelessly. She knew the penalty for murder, even at the tender age of ten.

Her family, along with others had been made to watch the punishments as a warning.

She remembered; the victims were dragged forward, thrown to the dirt, their necks stretched over the filthy piece of wood block. The executioner, awaiting with his large sword. The sharp sound as the blade whistled briefly through the air. The sickening thump as metal met flesh. The dull thud and the sorrowful, sudden silence as their screams died abruptly; whilst blood spurted from the still twitching trunk.

She reached up to her own neck; she remembered.

Suddenly, a flash of light, blindingly bright; a stranger materialized in front of her.

His clothes, regal; pose, majestic.

He was as a god!

She cringed in abject terror as he reached down to her.

"Do you understand what they say you did and what they will do," he asked in her own Chinese dialect.

She nodded slowly, stuttering, "They say I sliced a man's throat. I did not do it Sir. My shawl was stolen last night. Do you not remember? I saw you with it, in my dreams," she explained in between the sobs and hiccups.

He listened and nodded solemnly. Then offered salvation and eternal life in exchange for her power.

She quickly agreed, believing she would be reunited with her parents.

They signed the oath in blood.

The guards did not see him as they came to drag her out to the executioner. They had heard a slight chuckle from the dark corners of the empty room, which hastened their exit as they warded against the evil they felt.

Little Lian, kicking and screaming begged for mercy. Called to the Magician for the salvation he promised.

They held her small head down on the gory block. The flies buzzed in anticipation of another meal.

Her father shrieked and cried, her mother collapsed as Lian's head separated from her torso. Blood spurted as it hit the dirt and rolled obscenely towards them. Her brown eyes wide in horror and the mouth open with her last cries for Momma choked within her throat.

The Magician, now filled with the energy from this innocent child, spat and cursed Lian's spirit to roam for all eternity.

He slowly dematerialized, looking for his next victim.

"JUST A DREAM."

It was a typical old 1950's style diner; the chrome was dull and the glass, well, not exactly clean. I found myself sitting alone in the booth against the back wall that allowed me to watch people come and go while I sipped coffee. Several booths covered in beige plastic were scattered, interspaced with tables. They looked well-worn Formica with heavy wood chairs. Twelve dull chrome finished stools lined the counter, each covered with faded red plastic.

Two of the tables held patrons; a young couple ate at one, occasionally looking up at each other with love in their eyes. It made me a bit jealous.

The other held a family of four. The children were young and noisy, but not bothersome. It brought back memories of taking my sons out for breakfast or to the fast food places for dinner.

Three people occupied stools at the counter.

The griddle sizzled as the cook dished up to the food-awaiting servers.

It was a homey kind of place - old, worn, but pleasant. Jukeboxes hung walls at each booth with a mixture of the oldies.

Carole King was telling me, *'You've Got a Friend.'*

I daydreamed until a tap on my shoulder caused me to turn abruptly and look up.

There you were.

4

"It's nasty out there, Frankie," you cited with a smile, putting your purse and umbrella aside.

I returned the smile and stood; a quick hug between two friends. "This was the only coffee shop for miles that served 'Mountain Dew'," I said nervously.

"That's a strange greeting."

"If I gave you the greeting I wanted, in about two minutes the staff would be pouring buckets of cold water and prying me away from you with a crowbar."

You frowned as I slid over to let you sit.

It was a bit awkward, our meeting like this. I don't remember all of what we spoke. You sat drinking your 'DEW' and I sipped coffee. You cried, and I guess I did too.

"Why are you holding my hand so tight," you wondered.

"This is a dream and when I let go, I'll wake up, you'll be gone and I'll be alone, again."

The *'Carpenters'* told us, *'We've Only Just Begun.'*

We spoke of unimportant events; and of what we would each do, now. We sat, listening to more music from our era, sipping from cups.

'Carole' was on again, reminding us, *'So Far Away.'*

I sat back to look at you; you smiled, I smiled and let go your hand.

I awoke, alone, but content.

CHAPTER 1

The entity wanted me, and being that I was now alone, that vile thing finally would have its chance.

It was mid-morning and I had just returned from burying my wife, Judy. The official cause of death was heart failure due to high blood pressure. That was partially true, her blood pressure was high and her heart did fail, but nowhere did they mention that she had literally been scared to death by an evilness haunting our home.

Now, I had always lived in haunted houses. For my almost 60 years, wherever I moved, the ghosts followed, and greeted us. My Grandmother followed me for years after her death, never malicious, never hostile, just there. Doors would open and close; lights off, then on. An occasional item tossed across the room to garner attention.

Then Judy brought home the Ouija Board. I refused to participate and tried to convince her that it was dangerous. She thought it fun and invited girlfriends over for a party.

They ignored the safe guards.

I begged them to spread salt around the board to contain any evil spirits, and close the portals after the sessions to bar the way to our world.

And Holy Water just in case.

It was, at first, fun for them. Sometimes, one of the girls moved the pointer just to scare the others. Other times it moved on its own in answer to a question. They called upon seemingly harmless specters over the few weeks they played, and retrieved some interesting information.

Then the threats started.

I was in my den, relaxed in my recliner. A small fire blazed while I enjoyed a classic 'Dr. Who' on the BBC network when the first scream grabbed my attention.

The air in the formal dining room seemed heavier as I ran in.

"What the hell is going on," I demanded in a sharp tone. I saw my breath and shivered from the cold.

Hearing my yell, several women jumped away from the oak table, one with a hand to her mouth. Another had covered her eyes in fright, two other's cried.

The pointer moved across the board of its own volition, mesmerizing me.

Judy clutched my arm, sobbing, *"Make it stop, Frank, please make it stop!"*

But it slid faster to those same three letters.

"What happened," I asked, still not able to take my eyes from the board.

Judy's hysteria was rising, she hiccupped the sentence, "We were - asking questions - and the board was answering, - just as before. The room got darker - the air heavier and so cold we could see our breaths. The hairs on my arms stood up. The pointer bounced a few times to get our attention. Then it moved, spelling out, "DO THIS!"

Now terror took her.

"What..." I hesitated; not knowing what she spoke. I repeated, "What were you supposed to do?"

With a whimper, she sobbed wildly and pointed to the board.

The indicator moved between the letters, 'I'-'E'-'D'-'I'-'E'-'D'-'I'-'E', faster and faster.

Holding my arm tight in panic, she screeched, **"MAKE IT STOP. PLEASE MAKE IT STOP!"**

I managed to get a hand free; picked up the plastic bottle and poured Holy Water onto the board. The pointer rose, emitted a loud, inhuman groan; a wail that brought hands up to ears with the knowledge that there was no chance to block the sound. It then subsided to a long drawn-out sigh.

I told the women the Blessing would keep us safe. The pointer crashed back onto the board, slid, stopped at the word, 'NO'.

Her friends left, making hasty good-byes. I instructed Judy to dispose of the board. That turned out to be my mistake; she hid it in a closet.

I should have burned the damned thing that night.

CHAPTER 2

After the funeral; after the last of the mourners had gone; I was alone, lonely. I sat idly at my computer. My eyes had begun to tear again as I remembered. It was my fault she was dead.

We didn't have the greatest of marriages, with discussions of divorce a few weeks back. Neither of us was happy; neither wanted the same things anymore. However, this is not what I wanted to happen; not the way I wanted it to end.

I glanced down at the monitor, and through misty eyes noticed the flashing light.

Messenger signaled.

A contact to help distract me from my lamentations.

I double-clicked to see who called, grateful; happy someone had time for me.

Joanna, our dear friend.

I had spoken to her briefly about Judy, and she offered her condolences. She couldn't make it out for the funeral. There were some things she just couldn't put off. I understood.

We four were great friends. But I couldn't tell all the details. I could not voice it just then. Even to Joanna; the words stuck in my throat.

Not that she would not believe; she was about the only person who would believe everything that had happened.

Her message read, *'Paul was killed in an auto accident this morning!'*

I needed to re-read it to fully comprehend what she had written.

In shock, I typed back: *'NO! WHAT HAPPENED?'*

Her immediate reply; *'Can't talk now, strange events happening. Please help?'*

'WHAT KIND OF HELP?' I typed back.

'Under attack. Bad things going on. Please help,' appeared on my screen.

'OKAY!' I tapped out. *'LONG DRIVE, LEAVING NOW. BE THERE TOMORROW EVENING. WILL TEXT WHEN CLOSE BY.*

IF YOU NEED ME, CALL.'

'Can't talk, afraid of the Witch, he is watching and listening.'

Then messenger shut down.

I sat, stunned. Paul was Joanna's husband. They were married for as long as Judy and I. We had vacationed together over the past several years. I liked Paul; he was a nice guy, and now he was dead.

Her phone went to voice-mail.

I was already packing for the trip. A door slammed somewhere in the house. I threw clothes and toiletries into an over-night bag. An inhuman groan caused the floor to vibrate.

A few incidentals into a small knapsack; a piece of furniture slammed into a wall downstairs. As I zipped the bags closed, the lights in the room flicked off and on several times.

I called my sons to say I was leaving, and as to where and why. They knew to watch the house, not that anyone would break in and live for more than five minutes.

A burglar broke in about a week ago while Judy and I shopped. The police reported the perpetrator screamed about dishes flying, doors that slammed and strange laughter from the floors. One door slammed and broke his leg. He crawled out; hysterical, demanding the police lock him away. It took us two days to clean up the debris.

Some people have watchdogs; I have 'attack ghosts'.

The living room chair slid across the floor, stopped directly in front of me. I grabbed my bags and laptop from it, then walked away.

The front door slammed shut behind me several times after I had locked it.

I phoned, text and messaged her to no avail; she either wouldn't or couldn't answer.

CHAPTER 3

You might think it strange that just after burying my wife of twenty-four years, I would run off to help another woman. But there were extenuating circumstances. Joanna and I went back a long-time, way back to our teen years.

We were once engaged to be married.

I loaded up with the large sized coffee; gassed the car and as the saying went; put the 'pedal to the metal'; it was going to be a rough ride.

The message and the drive brought memories back, unbidden, of the early 1970's. I'd felt we were destined to be together, but maybe not then, and maybe not ever if the stars had their way.

My older brother married Karen, Joanna's sister. That is how we met, 'sort of'.

"My sister is about your age and lonely," Karen mentioned. "Maybe you can write to her?"

So, I wrote, and Joanna wrote back. She was a gymnast and high school cheerleader. The typical girl next-door, with honey-blond hair and pretty blue eyes that made your heart thump and your face smile. We were three thousand miles apart, and we wrote again.

The weekly letter became 'the two a week letter'; this turned into the daily letter. I joined the Army and still we wrote. We exchanged all of our secrets, all of our hopes and fears. We poured out our troubles, our wants, desires and our hearts.

She inspired my poetry.

We announced our engagement without ever having physically met; I mailed her an engagement ring.

On the next Thanksgiving, we finally got together and enjoyed each other's company, never letting the other out of sight.

I nearly went AWOL.

We met again over Christmas. I was on leave and Joanna was visiting relatives far up north. I drove eleven hundred miles over two days, through snow, ice, bitter cold temperatures to spend a few days with her, only to find out our love was ill fated.

She claimed she loved someone else.

Devastation; depression set in. We had words; she returned the ring. We cried; we talked and then cried some more.

I needed to be sure; I wanted her to be happy.

So, I left!

I walked away!

It was a long and lonely eleven hundred mile drive home again that festive Christmas week.

After our long ago breakup, I wrote to see how she was, to see if she was happy. She never did respond. She never did marry that guy either.

We reconnected several years ago on FACEBOOK. I was new to the site and was increasing my circle of friends; looking for lost relatives and old school chums when she contacted me.

It was as if time stood still. It was 1971 again. Yes, we were both married; we both loved our spouses, but we were good friends all those years ago and the years didn't matter.

All this ran through my mind as I drove, again, another long-distance to see her. This time she was in trouble; someone or something might be after her and may have killed her husband Paul.

I stopped for gas.

I first met Paul back when we four vacationed together. We spent several days becoming acquainted and re-acquainted, and then several more vacations over the ensuing years as old and dear friends. Now, he was dead in an automobile accident. I wiped my eyes as I slid back into the car.

We all had many things in common, besides the obvious one. We had planned to start businesses together, to spend more time together, buy properties and live as close neighbors.

Many thoughts whirled through my mind as I noticed more headlights come on. The sun had dropped down below the trees as I pulled into a motel.

At my age, though my ego bristled at the thought, I no longer had the stamina for non-stop drives. Falling asleep behind the wheel would not be a good idea. Besides, a motel should be safe enough; I didn't think the entity could follow.

I hadn't slept much over the last few weeks, with fighting the supernatural, then Judy's funeral, and the guilt of not being able to save her.

I didn't think that evil thing could purposely harm me. More than once as I screamed, ranted and raved at it, it retaliated and threw things, and they would miss. One coffee mug flew right at my head, stopped inches away, then dropped harmlessly to the floor.

It could disturb me with knocks and noises, but it could not harm me directly, it seemed. So, a good night's sleep was what I needed.

The drive put me on edge, with the tension and the stress. I checked the INTERNET for information about witches. The diversion helped as I drifted off to sleep.

A long drive the next day would put me in Missouri.

I rose early, a quick coffee and then back on the road. I text, letting her know where I was, but received no reply. I assumed she would be busy with the funeral arrangements.

Later, I received one-word:

"HURRY!"

With pushing the speed limits, and some 'creative driving', four hours later I was in town.

Her last text was an address of a restaurant with no further explanation.

I parked and walked into a diner –

THE DINER.

The one from my dream.

CHAPTER 4

I took that same booth near the back, ordered coffee and a Mountain Dew. I was living a dream, or a nightmare. I sat; looked over the old familiar songs in the jukebox.

We had last vacationed together two years prior and it had been a long two years for us both. Joanna seemed tired and drawn as she walked over.

But the 'look' was still there, the one that got the blood pumping. Yeah, she had aged; the hair had a touch of grey. Those few extra pounds on her lithe frame helped her figure.

But those eyes; they were the same. The twinkle and sparkle that held the attention of whomever bothered to look still got the heart pumping. The few little crinkles meant nothing.

I stood and we held each other as if we would never let go.

The feeling was different somehow, better, more fulfilling.

The snide comment behind me I ignored; it was more important of what we meant to each other, the deep feelings we intuited, then what total strangers thought.

I heard her choke back a sob.

That was all right, I hated to cry alone.

We disentangled and sat opposite each other.

With eyes red-rimmed, "Frankie, if I told this to anyone else, they would laugh at me, shake their heads, and then have me committed; but I know you will believe."

"A Witch killed Paul," was her startling revelation.

I stared at her and double blinked.

"Yes! I'm sure," with a nod. "The doctor ruled it a heart attack and with Paul's history of heart troubles, they drew that conclusion quickly."

She took a sip of soda, looked at the glass, then up to me, "You remembered the Mountain Dew."

I also remembered Paul's heart condition. "So, tell me what happened," I prompted.

"My car had been in the shop getting new brakes. When the repairs were done, he dropped me off in his Sebring and I followed him home."

A moment's pause, her eyes went down in a quick remembrance, dreading what came next.

"He went sideways into oncoming traffic. I screamed. Then he slid back, almost as if a hand moved his car." She stopped for a breath.

"He lost control and at high speed, hit a tree head on." Now the tears rolled down her cheeks as she relayed the incident.

"What made you think a Witch caused this," I asked.

"His car didn't swerve to the side; it moved as if pushed, as though a child's hand moved a toy sideways. It left unusual skid marks. All four wheels showed the lateral movement and there were unaccountable dents in the doors. The police thought the indentations looked as if giant fingers grabbed the car. It was unnatural."

She sat crying as the emotions flooded from her.

"I jumped from my car, ran to him. Twisted metal and glass strewn the ground, I tried yanking his door open. It was jammed; wouldn't budge. I smelled gas and hot metal."

Again, a pause; the look of sorrow crossed her face.

"I panicked! I didn't know what else to do. I cut my arm reaching in through the broken glass. I had wanted to pull him from the wreckage, through the window."

"Frankie, I was frantic. My Paul was dying, and I couldn't help him."

Her head sagged, a ragged breath to regain herself, to quiet her voice.

Several patrons glanced our way.

As her story continued; more tears rimmed her eyes.

"He stopped me, looked over, very pale; panic in his voice. He clutched at his chest. He knew there was little time. The pain etched his face."

"I screamed for help."

"He gasped, grabbed my hand, *'The bastard Witch is back, have to stop him'*."

"He coughed. A slight smile; a drop of blood dripping down his lip. He whispered, *'I Love you'*."

"Those were his last words."

I let her cry a moment then handed over a napkin to wipe her eyes.

"I heard a small titter near the front of the car, by the tree," she said in a raspy voice looking back up at me. "It was difficult to see through the steam and smoke."

A nervous sip of her drink.

"Nevertheless, in the crowd that had gathered I saw that bastard Gregory. He had threatened us years before, and now he was here." Her head dropped to her chest in sadness and fear.

"Then I got lost in everything. The police pulled me away. The firefighters forced open the door with some big tool and they took him from the car, to work frantically on him."

"They tried to hide the terrible truth. I saw an EMT turn and shake his head to his partner. When I looked back around, the witch was gone."

As the story unfolded, her hand grabbed mine and held on.

The waitress came back to take our order.

I looked at Joanna, "we should eat something."

She declined.

I tried to lighten the mood and insisted. "If we are going to be 'witch hunting', we need to eat."

The waitress gave us a strange look when I mentioned 'witches'.

With a thankful smile, Joanna ordered.

We sat and spoke more of the accident. I was trying to realize just how much power was needed to cause a car to crash.

"What are the hours of the services," I wondered, reaching for my cell phone to check the time.

"Seven to nine tonight," she informed me. "They recommended a closed coffin."

"Why? Was he that badly disfigured?"

"No, they said it would take an extra day to remove the look of terror from his face." A slight pause to swallow before continuing. "I took one night since there would not be many people. My children cannot make it, a few neighbors may show plus his co-workers. I notified the Veterans groups since he served in the military," she stated in a quiet voice, almost as if on autopilot.

The waitress returned with the rest of our meal, asked if there was anything else while removing the salad bowls. I looked to Joanna; a slow head shake.

"When we finish, I need to find a motel," I mentioned.

Her head snapped up. "NO," coming to her lips abruptly. She paused, looked around with a breath and a stutter, "I, um - thought you would use the guest room?"

"Do you think it appropriate?"

"I don't give a damned what's appropriate. I'm just too frightened to be alone right now," she replied sharply.

A few heads turned our way, curious.

I nodded, "I know what you mean. We'll drop off my bags and then head to the funeral home."

"We do need to move carefully," was the caution. "He wants me; my powers," she whispered.

"We shouldn't speak of it here," looking around at the people that had filled the diner.

She also looked, amazed at the number of patrons that had entered without our noticing.

As we ate, she looked up, "you told me little about Judy," pausing with a sorrowful expression. "What happened?"

I began the story of the events that night with the Ouija, and then. "Judy had been on edge for several days; ever since that incident. I would come home and she would be in tears, afraid to stay alone in the house."

"Relenting, I let her call the local priest. I knew he wouldn't believe what we were going through, and once he got there, would not be able to cleanse the house." I stopped for a breath and a sip of coffee.

"He showed up in his vestments, with Holy Water and an Altar Boy to help. They moved through the house, blessing and praying as they went. Half way through, the laughter started. Deep, menacing, and maniacal, it made the hairs on our arms stand up. The air grew thick with a deep, cloying feel. He continued the Blessings to my surprise, at least for a while longer. The Altar Boy cringed at every little sound and movement."

I picked up my coffee cup.

"They got as far as our bedroom when the closet door slammed, the wall shivered; a deep voice commanded, *'GET OUT!'* along with a few other suggestions. I think the boy wet his pants."

"The priest didn't need another invitation. Sweating and grunting they ran from the house; calming little until they were safely in his car and it in gear. He warned us to sell the house, to not look back, and… never to call him, ever."

I took a breath, an almost sigh.

She knew I had to talk about it, to get it out, to tell another person of my grief, my troubles. It helped to be able to face it and solve whatever the problem was. Moreover, no one else would believe.

"We had a psychic come in that last afternoon. I wanted to at least find who or what we were dealing with."

"She didn't find anything," Joanna told, more than asked.

"The poor woman barely made it through the door." Shaking my head slowly.

"She covered her ears yelling, *'NO, GET OUT OF MY MIND.'*"

Another pause to dab my eye and a taste of coffee. "She ran down the sidewalk, screaming for something to leave her alone."

I hesitated while the waitress refilled my coffee and left the bill.

"We were watching television later that evening when a moan started, a wail, really. It rose in pitch and volume, as if someone in anguish; it grew in intensity, hurting the ears," I told her.

"From, where," she looked, questioningly.

"It came up through the floor;" pausing a moment, "we don't have a basement if you remember," I said chuckling.

"The hairs on the back of my neck rose. The furniture on the deck flew out into the yard. I couldn't take anymore."

"Judy screamed in terror for it to stop. She begged me not to leave her, not to go. I ran out anyway, to confront this damned monster."

"Me; the *big hero*."

I paused to get control back. With a quick look around, I began again, a little quieter.

"It was a mistake. The sliding glass door slammed shut behind me, the lock clicked tight on its own, I knew we were in trouble."

Joanna's eyes grew wide.

"I tried to get back in, the door wouldn't budge. I used a wood bench from the picnic table to smash the glass. It wouldn't break."

"I screamed for the evil, son of a bitch thing to leave her alone."

My eyes were tearing.

"I stood, plastered against the glass, watching, screaming, crying. I pounded on the door to get in, to get that monster's attention. I couldn't tear my eyes away. Judy sat, terrified, pleading for me to save her."

"I yelled for her to run, to hide. She moved from the couch towards me, reaching out; reaching for me to save her. The horror on her face will stay with me for all time."

"Something grabbed her from behind, an unseen force. It slammed her to the floor. She lay a moment, then slowly rolled to her hands and knees and tried to crawl behind the sofa."

"I banged on the glass, again trying to distract or draw it away."

"The walls moved as if breathing. I thought I saw something crawling under the paint. I dialed 911, screeched that someone had broken into my house; locked me out, my wife trapped. I needed police and ambulance, please, now."

"I threw the phone, picked up the bench again, and mustered all my strength for one last, desperate try. The wood splintered in my hands on impact, the glass imploded, shards scattered throughout the room."

I stopped to sniffle.

"It was too late. She lie on the floor, gasping; clutching her chest. The tears ran down her face making tracks through the white dust from the wall plaster. It caused her already grey features to seem even paler. The forlorn look told me there was no hope."

"The police broke down the front door; found me crouched next to her, hysterical, crying. The EMT's rushed in, not even worried if the supposed perp had been subdued. They worked feverishly as I explained what had happened."

I stopped again, my voice quivered; my free hand shook as Joanna had hold of the other one. My tears fell upon the tabletop.

"They didn't believe you, did they," she asked, with a knowing glance.

"No, not at first," I began.

I got a questioning look.

"The EMT's worked on her, but the equipment failed; new batteries died; the lights flickered off and on. The oxygen worked because that didn't need power. No one understood what was happening."

"We heard thumps on the stairs; someone running up and down, somewhere a deep laugh. The police demanded I tell them whom I was hiding. The EMT's nervously tried to work on her even though they knew there was no chance." I sighed and continued.

"They would look over their shoulders feeling something dangerous. One volunteer eventually remembered being here the previous time with the burglar.

Eerily, a voice screamed, '*GET OUT*".

"Dust swirled, a closet door crashed open, clothes and articles flew, danced, and dove at us."

"The last straw was that laugh. It came from everywhere and vibrated every part of our being, sending chills through our souls. They picked Judy up and ran; the front door smashed shut as we narrowly escaped injury."

"We stood on the front lawn, looked back towards the house; it quivered."

"Then they believed," she asked.

Sitting back, lifting my coffee cup, "Then, they believed," with a shaky hand, I sipped.

Joanna still held my other hand.

CHAPTER 5

It was time to leave. She wanted to be at the funeral home before anyone else, to have a last time alone with Paul. I knew well that feeling.

The service was simple, quiet. Music played in the background; Paul's favorites from the 70's, from when he was young. The Veterans group did Military Rites at the flag- draped coffin. A few of his friends and co-workers attended, telling her how sorry…

She was cordial to all, quiet and subdued. We had set up a signal that if anything peculiar happened, any sign that Gregory was trying something, she would let me know or tell me if he made an appearance.

I turned to her after the Veterans had finished. "Just knowing Paul these last few years on vacation, I grew to love and respect him, like a younger brother."

I gave her a short, hand-written page. She looked down to read the quick tribute I had penned.

I went on, "We had many conversations about the future and what we all could do once retired. And now, his dreams have ended," I finished in a whisper.

I watched the tears flow down her cheeks as she handed back the page.

"You will read this now, for him?" The look on her face said I should not refuse.

I signaled to the minister who was conducting the service and explained the situation.

He graciously called everyone's attention and introduced me.

I stood at the podium, "I knew Paul only a few short years, but he became a very good and close friend. I would like to read this little prayer I just wrote."

"Dear Lord:
Our friend has now passed from us,
And we take him to his rest.
Please Lord, judge not harshly,
He has surely tried his best.
In the time that you've allotted
He's accomplished many good things.
He's had laughs, and yes, he suffered.
To You now his soul sings!
He has helped us all, Lord,
In many different ways.
And now, he's just a memory,
But a memory all our days.
So, bless this man, Your servant,
Whom you have deemed fit to call,
His job here is finished.
But I'll miss my good friend Paul!"

As I walked away from the lectern, there was complete silence, and then a few quiet sobs to tell me the piece, though simple, was the right sentiment. Besides, he was my friend and I felt I needed to say that.

With a soft pat on his coffin, I walked out the side door to the fresh air.

The remainder of the evening went without incident and shortly after nine; with a final goodbye, we left. There was not to be any other services. She would spread his ashes in the mountains that they both loved.

A short drive to her house and I walked a quick security check of the grounds and then did the same for inside. I still didn't think Gregory would attack her outright. There was too much chance of jail time, stalking at the very least, manslaughter if they could prove it.

She brewed coffee, knowing we would spend time talking.

I needed information, knowing I did not know enough about Witches.

CHAPTER 6

We got comfortable at the kitchen table.

"Let me start at the beginning," she suggested. "Many years ago while living in Florida, I needed to learn more about my abilities."

Looking at her curiously, I bade her to go on.

"You know I am a witch," she stated plainly, "and have always been one. Back when we dated, I didn't know. When I married Paul, I discovered my powers."

"I knew about the witchcraft, but explain more about your abilities?" Thinking it an obvious request.

"I can feel the future, sense vibrations; changes in and around us," she explained, "Nothing stupendous. I couldn't tell you what the lottery numbers would be; but I could sense when bad situations would arise."

I got a quick smile and a nod, "Yes! My senses were firing that day. I just did not know what to expect. So, it surprised me when I saw Gregory by the car," she explained. "We thought we were rid of him years ago."

"You never told me much about him. Why would you try to get rid of him, and why would he want to kill Paul," I asked, pouring more coffee.

"He had promised to teach me how to use my talents to foretell the future. He made many promises those few weeks that were never kept," a tired smile spread across her face.

"Maybe you want to wait until tomorrow to finish this story," I checked, "You look wiped out."

"No, I think that it's important to tell it now, while I am still upset. Tomorrow, I may not get a chance to relate all the important details. Let's go on if you can stay awake." A bit of a laugh, "I forgot what you went through to get here, and what you have had to deal with."

"It's the reason, I think, we are together again," I reminded her. "To help each other get through the sorrow and pain, to help each other survive."

She continued, "There was much I needed to learn about witches, back then."

"A friend took me to a fortune-teller on a whim. The Gypsy was good; saw my aura and immediately knew what I was."

Joanna was up on her feet looking for something to do.

"Do you want to eat," she smiled at me, "I make a mean omelet."

"Okay, if it's no bother."

"None at all; it will keep me busy, occupy my mind, maybe give me a few minutes where I forget what has happened?"

Eggs and butter came out of the refrigerator, a few onions and mushrooms, and the cast iron skillet went on the stove.

"Do you want help," I offered.

"Just sit and relax. The kitchen isn't big enough for two cooks at the same time," she half laughed. "Paul and I found that out ..." a gasp, her head went down; shoulders slumped in despair.

I jumped; my arms immediately encircled her while she wept, and she held on to me for dear life. I eventually freed myself. Her hands went to her face to weep again. I passed tissues and walked over to care for the omelets.

"Oh, God," she wailed. "He is gone, isn't he?"

She looked near to hysterics. I stayed close and let her cry for a while. To mourn helps; it's good to get the pain out. You never really heal, but it does help you to accept.

I haven't gotten to the acceptance stage yet.

I portioned the eggs into two plates and hunted up silverware; poured more coffee and retrieved a Mountain Dew from the fridge while she went to compose herself.

A few short minutes later she returned wearing a tough looking smile. There had been difficult situations before which she survived.

And would again, with help.

"I have tried to stay strong through the last few days; not knowing when Gregory was coming for me. Now, when I need to be the strongest, I find myself breaking down." She spent another minute to get control.

I offered my hand for strength, willingly this time.

Then she smiled as if something remembered caught her attention.

"Did you see it," she asked.

"See what," I wondered.

She rose and walked to the wall where a small plaque hung. Returning with it, she placed it in front of me.

"That poem you wrote when we had a problem with the house a few years ago. All the difficulties we faced, and you and Paul on the phone for hours to come up with answers and solutions.

I looked down at a beautifully framed copy of 'HOME,' printed on heavy, fancy paper.

"You knew how stressed I was," she continued, "And you said you would find a way to help, to let us smile again. Paul was so impressed that he copied and framed it. I know it by heart"

<u>HOME</u>
"HOME IS MORE THAN JUST A BUILDING
BOUNDED BY FOUR WALLS.
IT IS A FEELING OF WELL-BEING
WHERE COMFORT AND SAFETY CALLS.
YOU CAN HANG YOUR HAT AND COAT
UPON ALMOST ANY CHAIR,
OR TOSS IT TO THE COUCH OR FLOOR;
DOES ANYBODY CARE?
KICK OFF YOUR SHOES AND WALK
AROUND IN YOUR BARE FEET;
THOUGH IF YOU WANT, GOING NAKED
IS ALSO KIND OF NEAT!
IT DOESN'T REALLY MATTER,
IT IS YOUR PLACE WHERE YOU CAN DO
THE THINGS YOUR HEART DESIRES,
BUT THAT, YOU ALWAYS KNEW.
SO, SETTLE BACK, ENJOY THE DAY,
PICK OUT A GARDEN GNOME.
ENJOY ANOTHER MOUNTAIN DEW...
THERE IS NO PLACE LIKE HOME!"

She recited it beautifully; I was impressed.

I reminded her, "I heard the stress in both your voices. What, with the roof leaking, the cement patio cracking, the asbestos and the heater going on the blink," I finished, taking a sip of coffee. "It was the least I could do for such dear friends."

The emotions of remembered events of what had happened over this past week started my eyes tearing. Her hand reached out to grab mine for a moment.

As we ate, she finished telling me the rest of the experiences with Gregory.

"The Gypsy woman recommended that I see a Witch. My first thought, I was to see a woman. But then I met Gregory."

"We talked, he hypnotized me; said it was simpler to align my powers that way."

"Each time Paul picked me up to go home, he complained that I appeared tired, ornery, and argumentative. I didn't realize it; nothing seemed different. I had less energy, but Gregory explained that was my Chakra, my powers realigning. This went on for a few weeks."

"After one long session, as I climbed into the car, Paul grabbed for my pocketbook. Not knowing what he was doing, I pulled it away."

"He stopped me with his palm up, motioned me to wait as he removed his little tape recorder from my purse, and pressed rewind."

"As we drove, I heard the machine replay the conversation with Gregory. I wasn't happy with Paul spying. We fought; I yelled about his trust of me. He said it was not a matter of his trust of me, but distrust of the witch."

"After a brief argument, I quieted enough to listen to the rest of the tape. I heard Gregory send me down into hypnosis, then, align my chakra. With that done, he began something different, a spell to remove power from a conduit."

"I did not remember that part of the ritual. I heard him remove more power from me; more than was normally good to remove at one time. The next part was even stranger. He told me *'Paul is not good for you as a mate'. Do what you must to turn him away. Find ways and means to argue so he will hate you and leave.*"

"He also said how much better life could be with a true witch for a mate. Then I heard the post-hypnotic suggestions; to fight with my husband, put off sexual advances and for my conscious mind to forget all knowledge of the events of the session."

She rose to take the now empty dishes to the sink.

"I was livid, to say the least. I wanted to turn the car around, go back and smash his head. I wanted Paul to beat the crap out of the man, doing serious damage to his chakra." She smiled an evil grin.

"He calmed me down, said we had to think before we acted."

"He was right. I had no idea how much power Gregory had, or who his friends were. We could be in serious danger if not done properly."

"I saw his white-knuckled grip on the steering wheel, knew he used all self-control to not make a U-turn and go back. You remember his temper."

She stood quiet at the counter; the water running in the act of washing dishes, lost in remembrances. After a few extended moments, I cleared my throat to bring her back.

A sad look crossed her face glancing over at me.

"Well, anyway, we decided to drop a copy of the tape and a note to him saying that I would not be returning. He was not to contact me in any way."

A quiet sigh, "I wanted to mail it, but Paul needed to be sure the damned witch received it. He went in alone that next day. I heard him yelling and screaming, heard him threaten that any further contact would not be advisable. I won't mention what other consequences he promised."

She laughed a little at the thought, walked the few steps to the table, and took a breath with a sip of her Dew.

I sat, waiting for her to continue.

"We thought that would be the end of it and continued on our normal routine. We went grocery shopping." She gave a funny little laugh.

"As we pulled out of the parking lot with our purchases that Witch stood menacingly at the exit, an evil look in his eyes as we passed. Paul wanted to stop, confront the bastard. I pleaded just to leave, speed away. We did."

Joanna paused again, remembering the events, her eyes widened and her nostrils flared in fear.

"It virtually cost us our lives. As we picked up speed, the steering locked and the gas pedal went to the floor. Paul fought it, tried to wrench control back. He tromped down on the emergency brake and shut the ignition off."

"Nothing worked," she swallowed hard, the memory vivid.

"We careened off the road, bounced down an embankment and plowed into a tree. All that saved us from dying was the high grass and soft dirt."

"The big Chrysler Imperial protected us enough to cause just minimal personal injury but the car was totaled. The police had it inspected to find the cause of the accident."

Another deep breath, again to get control of her emotions.

"What did the mechanic find," I queried.

"He said there was no way that car was still moving with the emergency brake engaged as hard as it was. The brake pads had ground to powder and the mechanisms had melted from the heat due to the excessive speed. He also mentioned that the accelerator cable snapped under the hood, causing it to jam the throttle open."

"He swore that in all his years as a mechanic, he had never seen that happen. He had no logical explanation for those events or the accident."

I watched as her eyebrow shot up in a questioning stare, seeing disbelief on my face.

"I was sure you would believe me," she said with an angry air.

"What?" I retorted.

"You don't believe the story? You don't believe me?" She was becoming hostile.

"It has nothing to do with believing you," I soothed. "I have a problem getting my head around someone who could wield that much power. I need to research warlocks, wizards, and witches. There must be a way to protect ourselves from their powers?"

"First, there is no such thing as a Warlock; it's a misnomer," Joanna schooled. "They are witches, and second, I haven't come across many protection spells. What helps is we know who threatens us."

I interjected, "The term 'Warlock' denotes a traitor, or oath breaker, doesn't it? He has broken his oath as a witch from what you have said about him, so I think in this case, it would apply?"

She considered me, wondering what else I knew.

I shrugged; "I read a lot of books."

I saw her yawn and caught myself doing the same, "I think it's time for bed."

Stifling another yawn, Joanna laughed and nodded.

I suggested, "The living room couch would be a better place for me to sleep, just a short hallway down from your bedroom door. It's important to be near each other in the event something occurred."

She gave me an odd look.

"I don't know much about magickal powers. I want to be near in the event he attacks, and we can help each other ward him off."

Then after a moment of thought, I added, "It has nothing to do with feelings or affections. It has to do with safety."

With a crooked smile and a deep sigh, she announced, "Just so you know, Paul and I, although we loved each other, talked of divorce."

I gave her a nod to go on.

"It just wasn't the same. The fun and excitement had gone out of our relationship; the familiarity was not going to be enough to last through our old age. I just thought you would want to know. I still loved him and will miss him deeply, but we were to file papers next month," A wry smile as she walked down the hall.

"You know where the bathroom is and I'll get blankets and pillows," over her shoulder

I went upstairs to the spare room to get a few personal items from my overnight bag. By the time I returned from the bathroom, the couch had been made up; she sat there, waiting.

"Frankie, I just want to say thank you for coming to help. I had no one else to turn to. Judy was my friend and I am sorry for all that has happened. I know I didn't express myself that way earlier."

She got up to leave. I took her hand lightly as she passed, causing her to pause.

"I know what you thought of Judy and appreciate the sentiment. It will take time to get over the loss. I did love her; but like you, we talked of divorce."

I went on, "It had changed, we had changed; our likes differed; we didn't have the same goals anymore, or the same enjoyments. We hadn't mentioned anything to the kids; we were waiting until after all the holidays."

I checked the locks on the windows and doors before getting comfortable on the couch. I lie there for quite some time thinking, *"What have I gotten myself into?"*

CHAPTER 7

Morning came soon enough.

And in the sunlight we noticed nothing out of the ordinary.

She planned to scatter Paul's ashes in the mountains.

In this part of the country, winter comes early and at times without warning. Holding Paul's memorial in the snow was not a great idea.

I suggested we go today, now. The sun shone and the air felt warm; we might not have another chance before Gregory appeared.

We discussed various topics during the drive, from energy nodes to the size of pentagrams; the difference between new moon rituals and full moon services. The hour long ride flew by and my head spun from all the information as we pulled into the parking lot.

We hiked along, passing the small café where she and Paul had eaten.

"We could stop on the way back and grab a bite," she suggested.

"It's up to you if you think your emotions can handle it." I answered.

The spectacular scenery through the wide, smooth trail made the walk an easy one, boding well for me; as getting a bit older, my ego didn't want Joanna to think the walk too strenuous. I carried the backpack with waters, snacks, and her husband, Paul.

The trees swayed in the slight breezes as I caught a whiff of scents, maybe a mixture of pine and wild hyacinth. Off in the distance, a myriad of colors dotted the landscape adding to the majesty of the scene.

Although beautiful, I would not want to hike these trails after sunset. Large paw prints were scattered about the trail, maybe mountain lion or bear. Either one would not be safe to meet here, alone.

We reached the top, found the vista for which she searched and stood in the silence of the forest. The sanctity of nature encircled us like a comforting hug. The valley spread before us, her tears flowed as she remembered.

I offered a bottle of cool water while she explained they were here just last week to discuss the divorce.

More tears ran and I placed an arm around her shoulder. She sobbed and shuddered; her hand grasped tight to mine.

I cried; a tremor ran through me as I held my own vigil for Judy.

We stayed that way for some minutes.

This was the time to mourn, with the beauty of the surroundings, the care of a friend nearby.

Finally, both of us emotionally wrung out, I handed Paul to her. The breeze stiffened, the direction changed, now coming from behind us, as if in expectation.

She opened the box, reverently tilted it, spilling its contents.

And we watched as the ashes danced on the air, carried down, swirling towards the valley floor below.

She handed me the empty container, took a deep breath and walked away.

CHAPTER 8

The café was a twenty-minute hike.

We sat at a small table in the corner, held hands, and looked guilty.

We looked guilty because we felt guilty. The old feelings had resurfaced even though we both just buried our spouses. I was sure no one would notice, unless the staff recognized her without Paul.

We ordered a light meal and began to talk as soon as the waiter left.

"How much do you know about being a witch," I wondered.

"My knowledge is not extensive," she confided, "I learned some from Gregory on shielding and using a spell, but it isn't enough to go up against him and his powers," she finished on a downward note.

"I think we may have to find a bookstore. We need to educate ourselves over the next few days," I recommended.

"That sounds like a good idea but we don't have days. By tomorrow he will need to make a move against me," she warned. "He wants my power. He cannot regenerate his energy at the rate I can. For me, it's an automatic, like breathing. For him, he has to wait for the moons to recharge his crystals," sitting back, the tea cup in her hand.

"And what type of moon...when," I probed.

"The soonest will be the new moon, tonight," she answered and sat forward again, placing her tea on the table. "He will be at his altar with his talismans, amulets, and stones recharging them. Tomorrow he will come looking for me to be his conduit to raw power." Her hand quivered slightly.

"Then we should head back to see what we can use as a defense. Naming him a Warlock is not flattering, but I do want to be able to tell him to his face and survive."

"I thought you knew nothing about Wicca and Witches," she reminded me.

"I had a chance to look up a little about it," I volunteered. "And I have read over the years. I didn't want to come out here a total idiot, so, I learned enough to know that I need to learn a lot more before we get killed by this man."

"Back home, I have books that may help," she offered, getting up from the table.

We reached for the check together but I grabbed it first.

"I'll get this one," I offered.

She smiled and nodded.

My education began as we drove back to her house; about chakra, Wicca, the use of stones and crystals; even that the color of the candles had different meanings.

That time spent was worth the one-hour ride. What she couldn't tell me was how to protect against one ornery witch who would stop at nothing to get what he wanted. His want of her in one piece was the good news, as a dead conduit does him little good.

We spent the afternoon and evening reading about Witches and their spells. We hunted through books and pamphlets. We traced old stories on websites, and ghosts on the internet.

Joanna even called that old gypsy woman who had first brought her to Gregory. She was dead. Killed just last week in an apparent theft under strange circumstances.

Now, more than ever we needed to find information and spells. Counter spells were on the list. But offensive spells could put us one up when we met that witch again.

There was not much to find.

CHAPTER 9

"Let's take a booth near the rear where it's quieter," I suggested.

Most of yesterday and for some time this morning we researched Wicca and off-shoot sects for protection spells, amulets, sigils; anything that might help against whatever this 'traitor' was going to throw at us. He had to try to make a grab for Jojo.

Funny, I haven't thought of her by that name since we were teenagers. Recently, since we began vacationing together, I thought of her as Anna. More out of respect for Paul, since that is what he called her. It also made me think of her as his wife, and not my old girlfriend and lover

We didn't take much time last night to eat; just enjoyed a light supper and a ton of coffee for me.

It was the New Moon; Gregory would have been busy recharging all his amulets and crystals.

The waiter brought our lunch and refilled my coffee.

Joanna had been telling me of the special candles when she stiffened, the color draining from her face.

"What," I whispered, concerned.

"Gregory -" was all I heard before a middle-aged man with long white hair approached our booth. He wore a black, three-piece suit, Crystals and talismans hung about him and rings adorned his fingers.

"Blessed be, my dear Joanna," he greeted, and with a slight nod of acknowledgment to me, dismissed me as inconsequential.

"I was so sorry to hear about the accident of your poor husband, Paul. What a tragic event," he said formally as he took her hand.

She hastily pulled away.

"Can I help you," I asked, with some hostility. "Is there something you wanted?"

We had talked over what to do if he approached us in public. She would accuse him of murdering Paul.

If she couldn't, then I would.

I saw her struggle to speak, the look of fear raced across her eyes.

"Joanna knows what you did," I whispered to him, not wanting to get innocent bystanders injured if I could help it. We had prepared for a number of spells that he might throw at us here in the diner.

He glared at me with furrowed brow. "And to what do you refer," he commanded.

I felt a pressure on top of my head. Almost as if someone tried to push past my skull.

I shook it off.

"You know exactly to what I refer," I answered back in that same tone. "You caused Paul's car to lose control. You killed him!"

He began shaking his head, to deny any culpability.

"She saw you leave the accident scene. She was there; following in her own car."

Joanna continued to sit, to stare Gregory down and slowly nodded.

"So, take your platitudes and phony condolences and kindly depart," I directed, now rising to emphasize my statement.

"Do not think this over," he threatened. "There are more ways than you know for me to get what I want, with or without permission."

"Are you threatening this woman, Warlock," I spat, in a louder voice. My hope now was to focus attention on us.

He shot me an evil grin, "You think you have knowledge," he sneered. "Take it any way you think, but I mean to get what I want, no matter what or who stands in my way."

The witch looked me up and down, took a step forward, menacingly.

"Are you threatening this woman," I said louder, standing up straighter, intimidation tossed aside. "I don't believe that you would come in here and threaten this poor woman who just buried her husband yesterday."

I stopped for effect, and for a breath.

"And now, you come in here and threaten my friend with bodily harm. *How DARE You!*"

With each word, I had gotten louder. My heart raced as I stood there and accused a witch of murder. More people in the diner had stopped to watch the tirade. Even the cook came from the kitchen, carving knife in hand.

Several patrons now stood on their feet, awaiting a signal to rush to help.

The witch looked around apprehensively, saw that I had witnesses and decided to retreat. "You'll not be rid of me so easily," he whispered, heading for the side door.

The manager came over to make sure all was well, not wanting an altercation in his diner. I assured him it was fine and he shouldn't call the authorities. That deranged man was harassing my friend. However, thank everyone for his and her concern.

The waiter returned with hot coffee and another soda as Joanna began to calm and, with a hold of my hand across the tabletop asked, "Was that the smart way to handle it?"

"Better here where we have some control and help. Now that I know what he looks like, and can gauge his intensity, we can manage," I explained. "But, are you all right, it looked like you were in a bit of distress."

"I felt the bombardment as soon as he walked in. He tried to take over my mind. If you had not been here, he might have been able to get me to go with him," she answered, hesitantly.

"But I am okay now. His anger caused him to lose some concentration, and you stepping in with your loud voice allowed me to shake off the rest of his control. Thank you." She smiled with a wan look.

"Is that what I felt banging the top of my skull, his attempt to invade my mind?"

She looked at me while I explained what I went through.

Then I continued, "He tried to spread himself too thin and didn't have the power. The next time he will endeavor to take control of your mind and there will be no question of his intentions. We will be ready for him," I smiled back.

As long as we stayed together, we would be fine, as he needs to hold back for fear of hurting her. If he severely injured her, she would be useless to him. We had the advantage, as it were.

We left the diner and returned to the house. The real downside was all we had were defensive moves; there were no offense type spells that we could wield. It left us that much more investigating to do.

I had done an inspection of her home security when I first arrived and recommended she call the alarm company for a much-needed update. They pulled up to the curb as we got out of my car.

With a brief consultation and a walk around the premises they promised to return early the next day to do an upgrade.

CHAPTER 10

It had already been a long day, and I needed to sit a while to think. We gravitated towards her back deck to enjoy the remainder of the sunshine, me with a good cup of coffee, her with her 'Dew'. There had to be a better set of plans to protect her from Gregory. More, I needed to clear up something first.

"What does this man want of you," I wondered in all seriousness. "I'm still not sure what happens in this witchcraft thingy."

"First-off, it is not a 'witch-craft thingy,'" she began to explain. "It is a discipline, a religion if you will. We worship the Goddess, Earth, from whom we get our powers and energy. We channel it through our bodies to perform actions, or spells, hopefully for the betterment of people. We call that 'Magick'. Some call it 'white magick'."

"Then 'Black Magicks' would be ..." I interrupted her while she stopped to take a sip of her drink.

"Black magicks", she responded, "would be magicks performed to the detriment of others. This goes against the beliefs or tenets of our teachings, which is, in simple terms, 'HARM NO-ONE."

"That I can understand," I said sitting up a bit straighter. "But what makes him need you?"

"He can channel power to do amazing things as he did when he killed Paul." She stopped to let that thought run through her mind.

"That didn't come out the way I meant to say it. The word *'amazing'* meaning Magicks of that magnitude. His problem is the amount of energy he uses; he runs through it quickly with trouble recharging."

"Think of it as a car battery; Paul did teach me a few mechanical processes. As the car runs, it uses power initially supplied by the battery; then the alternator takes over, recharges the battery and helps run the car. Gregory's charger is too small for the energy he uses."

She half-smiled, "He has crystals and stones that hold charges and can use those to supplement his power, but they rapidly discharge, taking much time to come back to full power. And some can only be recharged through special rites or on special nights."

She stopped for a breath and to think how next to explain.

"So, how are you able to help him?"

With a smile, "I have a large recharger built in, and little in the way to use that power in a spell. I am a conduit. Power users can tap in, draw off, and use my power. I can quickly assimilate the energy from the surrounding air, or from the 'ley lines' and keep recharging."

"Eventually, though, I tire. If too much energy is drawn over too short a period of time, I can become ill and possibly die."

She sat back, picked her next words carefully, "If he did it for good reasons, I wouldn't mind helping him once in a while. But, he sells his powers and spells for much money to perform black magick. If a client wants a promotion, he won't spell them more intelligence or a higher capability. He casts a spell for the supervisor to become too ill to work, or to die. Thus, the promotion happens."

"That's seems evil," I said offhandedly.

"Yes! It is, and that is why he can't find help. He's a 'psychic vampire'. Most of the power he uses comes from other than him, which is why he wears all the jewelry. They are amulets and talismans used to hold and channel energy. But they drain swiftly and need recharging often."

"Okay. If you don't want to help him, can you resist? Can he still draw from you without you knowing it?"

"He can, a bit, anyway," was her reply. "For the most efficient means, a witch would need the consent of the 'conduit' and be in close proximity. In touching range proves to be best. I can project power to a witch in another location, but some dissipates along the way."

And her explanation continued, "I can resist if I feel someone pulling energy without my consent. But like any other action, it requires power to do that. I eventually would be too tired to struggle."

We paused for a moment to watch a robin chase a bug across the lawn.

"So you can feel if someone pulls power from you." I stated plainly.

"That's the problem. It isn't static; it is constantly in flux. I pull from it for simple deeds, and it recharges from the air around me. I release a little to lower the level and it recharges; mostly done without conscious effort or thought, but, yes, at times, I can feel it"

We sat for a few more minutes, enjoying the afternoon sun and watched as another robin joined the first.

"So, that's what tipped Paul off that something else was going on when you were getting lessons from Gregory?"

"Yeah, He noticed that I looked drawn and tired. I was cantankerous, even for me," she laughed softly. "I would become ill for a day or two. I acted differently, almost as if I were a stranger."

"Then," I said, "he traced it back to Gregory and your lessons; placed a recorder on you to hear what went on."

"Yes! But that was years ago. Something huge must be in the works for him to travel all the way here from Florida."

I speculated, "Maybe he has new clients that require a bunch of spells and doesn't have the power to cast them."

"Or more than likely," she interrupted, "a client that needs one big spell right away and he doesn't have the crystals to empower it," coming more to an upright posture. "It probably means a lot of money, so he got Paul out of the way to have a clear charge at me."

"But wouldn't he know you would have fought him on it," I speculated.

"If I didn't know what happened to Paul, or even that Gregory had done the deed, I wouldn't expect an attack. He could put suggestions in my mind from a distance to trust and help him." I saw her shiver, "even to fall in love with him. Only because Paul and I were together that day did I see what had happened? Otherwise, I would not have known. But I will be on my guard now," she avowed.

"If we had sufficient crystals to protect you, could you charge them," I inquired.

"Sure. That's the easy part. Just holding them in my hand I can push power into them, or if I wore them. If we left them in the Closed Circle, or a Pentagram, we could charge them and they would hold that charge longer."

"A Pentagram? Isn't that used for Dark Magicks or evil spells," I asked innocently.

"There are two designs and are exact opposites of each other. The top point of the star faces up on the White Witch design."

She rose to boot her laptop, "We are going to need to learn as much as possible about setting up altars and Wicca Rites and such," she instructed.

The next few minutes she traveled the information highway.

"We can use Paul's workout space in the basement. Move a few of his weights out of the way..."

That started the tears to fall and she shook her head, fighting her emotions, fighting for control. I handed tissues and put my arm around her shoulder to lend support.

She patted my hand before wiping her eyes. "Thank you for being here. I..." She choked back emotion. "I didn't know whom else to call."

"Where else would I be? Friends help friends; and right now, we need to help each other," I suggested, looking at her, my eyes also a bit misty.

"Let's see what we need to create the Altar and Celebrate the Rite." She scrolled through a few sites, and clicked a button. The printer zipped out with ceremonies, lists and designs.

One of the seemingly more difficult items became the easiest. Because of her love of creating jewelry, the crystals and stones needed were found in her work room.

She had many of the other items, also. The herbs, wine and knives she kept for her own offerings. We would need to buy chalk and colored candles.

The chalk was popular at any toy store as kids used it in abundance in drawing on sidewalks and driveways. The candles would need to come from a specialty store. Thankfully, she knew of one nearby.

CHAPTER 11

We pulled up at the front of a care-worn structure of indeterminable years in an older part of town. I looked at the building, afraid it might collapse before we even got out of the car. She assured me, according to a few of her friends, this building and business had been here for longer than most could remember.

A faded, hand-painted sign announced,

"THE CANDLE SHOPPE".

With no great expectations, we went in. It was a strange and quiet place. The energy seemed gentle and soothing. After a moment, she sighed.

It was funny because so did I.

A young man walked from behind a curtain that partitioned the back room from the storefront.

"My name is Joseph and you are welcome," he smiled.

"What," I ask, perplexed.

"I heard 'sighs' from you both."

He looked askance and continued, "There is much stress and anxiety coming from your auras. You have recently under gone much trauma," he stated.

We looked to each other and Joanna spoke, "Are you familiar with a man named Gregory Rogers? He's middle-aged, long white hair, nicely dressed and wears an inordinate amount of jewelry," she asked.

A momentary pause, and the young man answered, "He had a severe look on his face as if he expected the world to bow before him and hand him everything?"

I smiled at that addendum to the description.

"You know him," I queried.

Joseph warned, "If you are friends of his, I will have to ask you to take your leave."

"No," she objected, hurriedly.

"Good! He came in looking for crystals and candles," he went on with the explanation. "I refused to help and asked him to depart. His energy vibrations caused me to do a cleansing before I touched what he might have handled. His negative spirit practically choked me."

Joseph stopped, looked at us both, and smiled. "I could tell that your negativity originated from outer means. Gregory's were self-made. He enjoys being a black witch. I wanted him out of our store."

Starting to feel very relaxed, I sighed again.

He pointed to a corner; stools, chairs and a giant stone clustered as a meeting area.

"That geode came to us via an old friend; I saved his life a time or three. He owned a mountain and left us that in his will," a touch of reverence in that statement.

"I am sorry for your loss," Jojo intoned.

"Come, sit, and be safe; you need shelter for a time; we will talk and see where we can help," he offered.

"We thank you, but we don't own any mountains," I joked.

"I know. That will be fine. If it is against this man Gregory, we will do all we can. Why don't you explain it?"

"But first, can I get you something, refreshments? Coffee, tea, soft drink, I am having Mountain Dew, myself." He continued smiling as he headed towards the curtain.

Joanna's eyes lit up at the mention of the soft drink. "Dew sounds great," she answered.

"Coffee please, for me, with cream, no sugar," I asked as he went through the curtain.

I saw her worried look. "Should we trust him? Was he telling the truth, or are these more lies for Gregory. Is Joseph as good a soul as he admits?"

"I don't know," I answered back with a thoughtful frown. "What are your feelings telling you? What did you feel when you walked in," I looked at her questioningly. "We both felt as if great weights had lifted from our spirits as we entered, I would go with that thought. I'll leave it up to you, though."

The young man returned, conversing with someone in the back room; telling about us. The other voice answered, feminine in tone, stated she would be out anon.

He brought a tray with the refreshments and an extra treat, cookies.

He nodded to them. "That was about what my wife Kyra was asking. She makes them from scratch, adding just a hint of mint; I cannot keep my hands off them. She hides them and then questions when I find and bring a few out.

We helped ourselves and I was pleasantly surprised with the treat. It was light, delicate, not too sweet and with just a hint of the mint and... cocoa?

My eyes went wide.

Joseph, who had looked up after taking a bite of his own cookie, chortled.

"See, I told you they were good," he winked.

Jojo enjoyed a bite or two and after a sip of soda began to explain the problem with the 'Warlock'.

Joseph's face darkened when she mentioned him trying to steal her energy. He was livid when he heard about Paul.

"These actions reflect badly upon all practitioners of the Art. It gives us Witches a bad name," he stated flatly. "What are you trying to do?"

"I want to hide my energies from him; hoping that by making it harder, he may just leave. I think he has an agenda and timetable. So, a few days of holding him off might do it," she finished.

A cat, seemingly from nowhere was at our feet. It sniffed her pant leg, looked up at me with disinterest, and with a tail swish, jumped into Joseph's lap.

It was a pretty cat; pitch black, gorgeous coat, and piercing gold-flecked amber eyes.

"It will not be an easy task," he began, as he petted the feline. "It will take much diligence to keep a black witch from tapping into your energies."

He sat scratching the cat, deep in thought. His hand rose to rub his third eye and his head snapped up, "Yes! That's the one, precisely," he announced looking down as the cat jumped to the floor. "Thank you," he directed to the feline.

It looked up, blinked twice and headed for the room behind the curtain.

He walked to a large cabinet at the back of the shop; rummaged for several minutes, stopped twice to rub his chin in thought as he searched; then, stopped again.

He took a breath.

I watched his shoulders shrug to ease the stress. He then walked across to the other side of the room, opened a small box, removed an item, and in a moment, was back.

"If I had just let my senses think, I would have found it immediately," he explained.

Shaking my head, I realized I had much yet to learn.

He held his hand out and there hung a small, but shiny dark crystal tethered to a piece of rawhide. It caught the light and glittered; eliciting shivers and sighs from each of us. It seemed both powerful and ancient.

"This will help refract negative energies. It should also help repulse any spell he may throw at you."

She took it in her hand and smiled with delight. It sparkled more.

"Just wear it as a necklace and it will help to hide you," he directed.

Handing it to me to fasten about her neck, I could not keep my eyes off it.

"You also need the candles, correct?" He put his Mountain Dew back down on the geode and called to his wife. "Kyra, please bring out that package and that bit of sage there."

I was just putting down my empty coffee cup when his wife came through the curtain.

"A bit of fresh sage for the altar; the fresher, the better to cleanse the room," we got up and walked to the counter.

Kyra was pretty, and I didn't mean to stare. She was young, lithe and smiled as she handed Joseph the package. They made a nice couple.

Looking right at me as she turned to leave, I couldn't help but notice the golden flecks in her eyes.

She blinked twice and walked back behind the curtain.

I stood with my mouth agape until Joanna asked, "Are you all right?"

That brought me back to the present. I shook my head and "Uh, yeah, sure, I think so," I answered bewildered.

She threw me a quizzical look. I smiled and said I would explain later.

He handed Jojo the bill. She studied it, puzzled; a troubled look upon her face.

"Um, Joseph, you didn't charge me for the crystal," she pointed out.

"It's not for sale," he told her without looking up.

Panic and bewilderment flashed across her eyes, not quite understanding about what he talked. She started untying the leathers to return the stone.

He stopped her with a motion of his hand. "You don't understand. It is not mine to sell."

Now we were both confused.

"If you didn't deserve the help of that crystal, you would not be wearing it. It would not have let me think of it, or even let me find it," he stated in all seriousness.

"When the time comes, you will know exactly of what I talk and know what you must do. That is all I can tell you, because that is all I know." He smiled wanly.

She paid the bill with a still unsure look.

I thanked him for the coffee and the help.

As he took my hand to shake it, "You two are inexplicably intertwined, and have been for many lifetimes, at a very deep level." He lowered his arm after letting go. "Your problem will ultimately solve her problem and in turn will solve your problem."

He shook his head as if coming up from a trance and stepped back with a smile.

"I really need to get that fixed," he chuckled.

Now we all wore perplexed looks.

Joanna and I walked back to the car.

"Then what was the problem in there with Kyra," she asked, "something about her troubled you?"

"I don't know what it was; she seemed to mimic the cat. She had that feel to her, a feline feel." I tried to explain.

"Many women have that 'feel'," she told me, smiling.

"Yet, the way she moved; she had gold flecks coloring her cornea, the same as the cat." I sat driving, a slow shake of the head and, "there is something not natural with that couple," I mentioned to her.

"You are talking about 'not natural'?"

"YOU?"

"Your wife Judy was scared to death by a ghost; sorry, may she rest in peace. My husband Paul died in a car wreck caused by a witch and you are speaking of not natural." She looked at me as if I had three eyes.

Well, technically...

"Yes, all true, but you didn't see the cat double blink to Joseph; did you? The last thing Kyra did was double blink at me. It was freaky. That is all I was trying to say."

"You are beginning to lose it, I think." She smiled again.

"Yes, I am." I kidded. "And for all the reasons you just mentioned, plus Kyra is Joseph's wife and, I think, '*familiar*'. I believe she is a shape-shifter."

"Some of the occurrences I have experienced this last week would make a great sci-fi novel; but I sure as hell hate to be living this."

Jojo agreed, and also agreed that it was time to eat. And since we had not been shopping, the lateness of the hour dictated we should eat out, again.

We chose the diner. With the frequency of our visits there these days, it had become 'our place'. Moreover, with the dream I had had, it was something else about which I would have to ask.

The same booth near the rear was empty and it was the same waitress as last night, who smiled; things were becoming familiar. It shouldn't have happened as quick as it did, but...

CHAPTER 12

We ordered beverages; her Mountain dew and my coffee came promptly; and we perused the menu looking for the one item that would get the taste buds salivating.

I decided on onion soup, salad, and an order of ribs. When in Missouri, one had to have the ribs.

A steak got her taste buds working.

There was much to discuss as we sat, awaiting dinner. Most couples would talk about their children or grandchildren, maybe a conversation about bills or a piece of furniture that needed replacement; while a few would sit and stare into each other's eyes, with murmurs of sweet words of love.

I don't think anywhere else in this entire world was there another couple discussing plans to thwart an attack by a Warlock; or beginning to devise ways to chase a demon from a house.

If it was a creepy, scary or insane conversation, I was there in the middle of it.

Our waitress, Janet brought platters and we paused in our talk.

In that continued silence, we began to enjoy dinner.

I reached for the salt.

"A man your age should be careful with that stuff," she cautioned. "Too much could kill you," laughing, thinking she made a joke.

"Yeah, I know," I replied. "Judy would remind me of the same ..."

A sigh escaped my lips before I realized I had even uttered it.

"Sorry," I stopped to catch my breath, "with all the other problems, I need to put my feelings away for now."

I put the salt back on the table, her hand went 'round mine to help quell the sadness.

"There is no time to put feelings aside. We have seen how fragile life is, and that, at any moment things can change drastically," she smiled sadly at me. "We need to live in the happiness of the moment, since this moment is all we have."

"You always seem to know the right words to say, Jojo," I smiled.

"Funny, hearing you call me that brings back happy memories." She paused in the discussion to spear a piece of broccoli. "Do you remember giving me that name?"

"Of course I do, even after all these years, I couldn't forget something like that," I admitted.

We had been writing to each other about four months when she complained about her name. Joanna seemed 'so formal and stuffy', she wrote. She wanted to change it to something simpler. 'Jo' sounded too much like a boy's name.

"I wrote you that poem," I recalled, smiling.

"You don't still remember that; do you?" She stared at me with amazement.

I stopped, took a breath to recollect a bit of the past.

> *"You said your old name*
> *Was much too stuffy;*
> *Just not quite your style.*
>
> *You wanted one that*
> *Was quick and funny,*
> *Adding more charm to your guile.*
>
> *So, with Love, pen in hand,*
> *I Paced and wrote, 'HEY JO'!*
> *With twice the feelings,*
> *And twice the LOVE,*
> *I christen you,*
> *ALWAYS...*
> *'Jojo!"*

Silly, yes; but written with love a long time ago.

We both laughed a little at the memory. It was bitter sweet, thinking of what might have been. The cards had dealt up a busted hand of love, I remembered.

We were rushing things Jojo said, she wasn't sure if she loved me enough.

I took offense.

After the breakup, we lost track, with moving, the military, getting married to others.

I regretted not running after her, chasing her, looking for her. The years we were apart were hard on me. I don't think I ever found another person who truly understood, or made me feel so fulfilled. I spent the next forty years remembering her smile and light dancing in her eyes. My other relationships never quite matched up.

We sat a moment longer, her hand on mine across a diner's table. Janet chose that moment to see what else we wanted.

Jojo shook her head and I concurred.

"No, thanks, dearie, we are both quite fed up," I answered, jokingly.

She left the receipt and walked away chuckling. I guess waitresses don't get much humor at work.

As I checked the tab, her phone rang.

"Hello," she answered. "Yes, this is her."

There was a pause as the other person asked something.

"No, we are out right now, is there a problem?" She let go a small gasp. "We can be there in five minutes, yes, notify the police." As her phone went back into her purse, our eyes locked.

"That was the security company. Someone set off the alarm at the house. The police are on their way."

We rose quickly, I handed Janet the bill and the cash, related why we could not wait at the register to pay. I included a large tip.

CHAPTER 13

Two police cruisers sat in front of the house with their lights on as I pulled up. Another was in the driveway, so, I parked in the street. An officer talked with her about what they had found. She unlocked the house and shut the alarm down, then waited by the front door while a sergeant, along with his partner went in to investigate.

I followed another officer around to reconnoiter outside, seeing what had set the alarm off in the first place.

He waved me to a side window hidden behind a bush; I saw immediately what had happened.

"Looks like a professional job, Sir," he commented; "see where the glass is cut in a circle and popped out, to not set off any vibration sensors."

The window slightly raised, the hole neatly cut; a quick look around and ...

... I removed an old business card from my pocket and slid it under the round piece of glass.

"Someone may step on it; I'll place it on the sill." I offered.

He nodded.

"Good thing you had the security clips engaged. It caused the perp to reach far enough inside to undo them that he knocked that stone off the sill. The motion set off the alarm," he concluded, as his light shone to outline the crystal in the middle of the floor.

The Sergeant, finished with his inspection waved at us to come in. We met in the kitchen.

After a quick confab with his officers, he started the explanation.

"I am Sergeant Adams. It looks like a professional job, Ma'am." He speculated, "And it fits in with other break-ins."

"Your husband just passed?" He questioned.

A brief slow nod from Jojo.

"I am terribly sorry." He offered condolences. "But the thief sees the story in the paper. Thinking you are not home, he decided it is too good an opportunity to pass because you are at the 'funeral home'." He paused for effect, "An easy target, a quick in and out and lucrative score."

"Um, Sir, You will have to re-set that alarm on the window. It looks as if he jumped the sensors. Jim, go with him in case he needs help. You have the expertise."

The officer acknowledged the Sergeants' order and followed me down the hall.

"Ma'am, it will just take a few minutes to file the report. I will have a dusting crew out in the morning to see if they find any fingerprints or other physical evidence. Just keep out of that room for now," he asked.

"We have an alarm crew coming in the morning to update the system. Frank suggested it after Paul died," she informed him.

"No problem, our crew will be in and out in just a few minutes. Just have them keep away from that window until we are through," he nodded to her.

With the sensors repaired, I left the jump wires by the piece of glass for the investigators. Jim was pleased with my work.

As I passed through the kitchen, I announced I would check around outside one more time. They didn't need me for the report. Besides, we still had the candles and supplies in the car.

The other officers had left while I finished checking bushes and the deck area. I carried the packages inside and placed them on the kitchen table as the Sergeant was just finishing. I offered to walk him out, wanting to move my car onto the driveway, anyway.

"There will be additional sweeps through the neighborhood," he assured me, getting into his cruiser, "just to be on the safe side."

"Thanks Sarge. I'll be here tonight again," I said, "I wouldn't feel right leaving her alone. Be careful out there," I cautioned.

He waved a 'thanks' as he drove off.

CHAPTER 14

When I returned, Jojo had arranged our purchases upon the table and was folding the bags. She stood with her back to me, staring at...

Turning at my footfall, our eyes caught and I heard a sob. Two steps to her and she was in my arms.

"Is this truly happening," she questioned through the tears. "Or is this a nightmare? A traffic accident caused by a Witch killed Paul; Judy died of fright because of an evil entity. I have a Witch chasing me; there's a demon chasing you, and now; some bastards try breaking into my home to steal my belongings after reading Paul's obituary."

Every few words punctuated with a gasp, a sigh, and more tears.

With tissues to daub the pain from her eyes, I tried to comfort whatever way I could.

She looked up at me; a sad smile crossed her face. "I must look a sight," she half-gulped.

"I think you look just beautiful."

Her eyebrow went up in a quizzical stare.

As I bent my head closer, our lips met, lightly, hesitantly; a quick taste of a kiss. Then separated; a quiet sigh, and then together harder, more fervent; putting forty years of desires into that one kiss; compressing a lifetime of old emotions into just one instant that went on forever, and was over way too soon.

After a short eternity, our lips parted. I looked into her face, wanting to say what I felt and had felt for decades and for just a moment, that same look stared back. As if ...

Then, the guilt took over, we broke the embrace; stood, awkward, looking everywhere but at each other.

"I think we'd better have a talk," she suggested.

"Good idea. I'll get us something to drink," I replied, sheepish.

We settled on the couch.

Placing the drinks on the coffee table I turned partially towards her to facilitate conversation. She looked as if she didn't know how to proceed.

But I did, "You are feeling quite guilty right now."

It wasn't a question. She nodded; eyes down.

"Me too," I stated firmly. "It is understandable. We both buried spouses whom we loved." I took a breath to get my emotions under control. "We are both under great strain, as you said earlier. Our emotions are running overtime. That kiss was not some little kid thing for the want of gratuitous sex. We both meant it because we both have deep feelings for each other. I felt that before the kiss."

I stopped to let her think. "Am I wrong in what I say?"

"No! Not wrong at all," Jojo agreed. "I think what happened tonight was inevitable, but it happened too soon. Events are moving too rapidly."

She sighed with that last statement.

And I continued, "Yes, they seem to be moving fast. I hope it is because we have a premonition of what good times lay ahead. I think, though, it was just the culmination of all that went on."

"Are there feelings between us? I know I think so, and I have always had them."

She paused for a breath and a sob, "and I know that I also have feelings, but I need time to sort them out, get them settled, Paul is gone just a few days."

"I know! No one is asking you for anything. The kiss happened. If we are together more, it will happen again. We are not here with promises to be forever faithful to each other. I need neither promise nor any action on your part. Whatever comes of this, will come. We will go on from there."

"You think I am putting too much into all this," she said in a serious voice. "Maybe I worry unnecessarily, but after what I have been through it seemed wise to keep it slow; with my emotions on the roller coaster they have been on." She smiled tiredly and advised, "Let's go down and set up these protection sites. We will need them to fully charge and protect the crystals."

We walked to the stairs. As I opened the door, her hand touched me shyly on the shoulder.

"I do know that you have feelings for me," she commented.

I stared at her quizzically.

Her one eyebrow went up again, "You haven't run screaming into the night."

"Yet," I joked, following her to the basement.

We set the crystals in place, but did not want to 'close' the circle until we were ready. I drew the pentagram. The altar, we set up as it should be, using all the diagrams and lists of items. With that complete, it was late and time to take a break; I needed coffee.

Afterward, I decided to bed down on the couch another night. The spare room upstairs was a long way to come if either of us needed help. She went into her room after somber and subdued good nights.

My mind raced. What would Judy think, what would she want me to do. Was I hurting her memory?

So many conflicting thoughts raced through my mind, keeping me awake.

I eventually did sleep.

Then, a hint of light streamed in through the shade I never closed after the check of the windows last night.

CHAPTER 15

I awoke and blinked. The clock read six thirty. I headed for the bathroom and a quick shower. Letting her sleep, I would awaken her later, to a good breakfast.

As quietly as possible, I searched out the fixings for the meal. Leaving the scrambled eggs a bit runny, I placed them in the warm oven with the bacon; the bread in the toaster, ready to burn.

I knocked softly upon her door and with no response; opened it, saw she still slept. A slight shake on her arm got a bit of a response, her brow furrowed, and mouth opened partially as if to form a question. Another shake got an eye open.

"A… who, what?" Then a slight smile and she was more awake. Reaching an arm up, and sliding it around my neck, she pulled me down for a good morning kiss.

I was surprised, delighted and not at all disappointed.

"Morning," she greeted me with that continued smile.

"Morning," I smiled a greeting back. "Now either you have to let me go and get up or the police and alarm company will be working around us while we make love all day."

Her lips showed a little frown, and then her face brightened as she asked, "all day?"

"Guess you will have to wait to find out," I joked.

She groaned and laughed as she sat up; the nightgown slipped, leaving little to the imagination.

I whistled.

"Cut that out," she warned with a grin. "The police will be here soon."

"Let them work around us," I suggested.

"Get out while I dress," she ordered, climbing from the bed.

"Yes Ma'am," I joked. "Do you want tea or mountain dew with breakfast," as I headed reluctantly for the door.

A questioning look came my way.

"While you slumbered peacefully, I engaged in the culinary art of breakfast making." I intoned formally; "Omelets with bacon, toast and your choice of beverage; I couldn't find potatoes, so no hash browns, sorry."

"Tea, please? Funny I didn't even hear you in the kitchen. I would hear Paul all the time ..." A pause, her eyes closed tightly, and a quick shake of the head. They reopened with a slight tear.

"Sorry, I did not mean to ... I ..." she was stammering.

I took quick steps, my arms enfolding her, feeling great satisfaction.

"*HEY! Hey, it's okay.* We will have many moments where thoughts and memories will come flooding into us, over-whelming our senses."

I sighed briefly to gain control of my own emotions. "We are in no rush. Any mention of Paul does not make me jealous. Let your feelings go where they may. I am here to help."

She took a step back and with a small tear in her eye, managed a smile. "Always the gentleman, aren't you?"

"To a lady such as yourself, yes," I bowed in courtly fashion.

Ten minutes later we were enjoying breakfast. The investigators knocked on the door and I showed them the room with the broken window.

We finished eating while they worked. An offer of refreshments graciously declined and very little time taken to complete their task. The preliminary report turned up nothing; no fingerprints showed; nothing left behind. There was no evidence of any kind. They said the 'perp' was that good.

The alarm company representatives arrived as the police were leaving which raised many questions by the Security crew chief. We assured them the alarms worked the way they should. The burglars did not gain entrance because the alarm sounded. They apologized again and went to work on the upgrade, now included was the replacement of the window sash. They had carte blanche.

Down in the basement, the altar needed the last few items and the pentagram still needed finishing. I was diligently drawing words on the floor when I looked up.

"Are you cold," I asked.

She gave me a quick look, "No! Why?"

"Because you're shivering," I mentioned.

"No! I'm fine," was her answer with a quiver in her voice.

During the next several hours I noticed the same reaction; a shiver, I questioned and she replied the same.

"Nothing is the matter," sometimes with a quiver, other times a weak smile.

By late afternoon, the alarm people needed to set passwords and run checks to the system.

She wanted me there with her to set them.

"Silly! You need to know them."

I agreed and we used simple numbers and letters pertaining to Judy and Paul's' name. It was nearing dusk by the time they cleaned up the debris and left.

It was too late to shop, so we decided to return to the diner.

By this time, we had labeled it 'ours'.

Our booth was empty and Janet was again there to serve. To make it simple, we ordered steaks, baked potatoes and salads. By now, Janet knew about the coffee and the 'Dew'.

We sat chatting about days of old, our children, and grandchildren, just general chit-chat to pass the time.

In between the talks and smiles, and the relaxing moments, she shivered again.

"You have been doing that all day," I mentioned. "Would you please tell me what is happening?"

She started to wave me off.

"No!" I insisted, "If something is happening, then I should know. What if Gregory is trying to cast a spell about you," I cautioned with concern.

"That's not it," she stated bluntly putting her hand up to forestall any more comments. "I keep getting the impression of Paul trying to reach me, contact me. I feel his presence; he wants to tell me something. He waves to me to follow - follow to the mountains, where - he is, where we - scattered his ashes."

"He keeps trying to say something." She talked slowly, paused to breathe, close to tears. Her hand reached out to no one, to a specter perhaps. She shivered again, let out a slight gasp, looked to me and a tear slid down her cheek.

"I need to go to him." She sighed softly, pushing the empty dish aside. I held her hand while she took a moment to compose.

Janet came to serve the rest of the meal. Picking up the empty salad bowls, she stopped; with a serious expression, "Is everything all right? Is your wife OK?"

I looked up and saw her concern.

With a grateful smile, I told her, "Yes, basically. As all right as it could be, under the circumstances, thank you."

I had a quick thought. "But, first, she's not my wife. I am a very old and dear friend. Her husband died in a tragic car accident the other day. I am out here trying to help."

"OH! How terrible. I am truly sorry," she intoned to Jojo.

And then to me, "Are you married?"

"Yes, no, well, I was. My wife died of heart failure about a week ago."

She showed me a strange look and backed away a step.

"No, it wasn't like that," I soothed. "Do you believe in the paranormal?"

"You mean like in ghosts and demons? Yeah, I-I guess," she answered hesitantly.

"Several weeks back, my wife Judy and a few of her friends unleashed a demon from an Ouija board."

"Wow! Those things are dangerous."

I watched her shiver at the thought.

"Just over a week ago, after several long and scary nights, we had a priest in to bless our home. The demon scared him out of the house. Several nights later it locked me out."

"Before I was able to get back in with the police and EMT's, my wife was lying on the floor, literally frightened to death by the entity. The police accused me of making up the entire story, and suspected me of murdering my wife. But then the entity tried to kill a police officer, ultimately chasing us all from the house. Even the investigators would not come near the place after that."

I finished my story and watched the goose bumps form on her arms.

"That was when Jojo called me to help her, and here I am."

"I think I remember reading about the car accident, it went out of control and hit a tree." A look of recognition came to Janet's face. "They said it was strange the way it happened," she mentioned.

"Yes! What the paper did not say was her husband died when a Warlock magically took control of the car and caused the crash. He wants Jojo for the power she can generate," I finished.

I watched her eyes dart from me to Jojo and back as I told the story.

"Wow!" A tight smile ran across her face, she shivered walking off.

Jojo's eyebrow rose questioningly as she chewed her steak. "Why did you tell that poor girl all that horrible stuff?"

"First, all the horrible stuff is real," I related, shaking my head, not believing what I just said.

"Second, if we need a place to come, a safe haven, this is it. They can't help protect against the magicks, but physical stuff, we can get help."

"But Janet is the only person that knows about it," she reminded me.

"You watch, by the time we leave, every person working here and a few of the regulars will know our story," I advised, spearing another piece of baked potato with sour cream. There was never enough chives.

She tossed me a wondering look.

"This is a small diner in a small town. Everything odd is big news and news travels faster than lightning."

We had settled down to enjoy our dinner when she looked up and stated plainly, *"I'm going."*

"Going where," I probed, startled at her demeanor.

"Going to the mountains to see Paul," she stated.

"Okay. We can do that. We'll go at first light," I suggested.

"No! I have to do this alone," she stammered, "and I am leaving after we eat."

"It will be dark by the time you get there," I cautioned her. "That path is dangerous enough in the light. You can fall off the mountain, slip, break a leg and die out there, all alone. A mountain lion or bear could have you for dinner. I can't let you do that."

"*I'm going,*" Jojo stated vehemently, spearing the last of her string beans. "And you can't stop me."

We decided to hold any other conversations for when we got back to her house. It was a long, quiet ride home.

CHAPTER 16

She began collecting items for her trip as soon as we went through the door. A flashlight went into a bag; a sweater followed.

I took her by the arm, "Sit," I motioned to the couch.

She looked defiant.

"You can spare a few minutes of your valuable time before going off to die, can't you," I wondered.

Shrugging, she sat at the edge of the cushion, ready to bolt if I said the wrong word.

"I want you to think about this for a moment," I held my hand up to forestall any comment. "Is it possible that Gregory is casting a spell to make you believe that these feelings are from Paul," I put to her.

"Could he be trying to lure you to the mountains to spirit you away?"

I wanted her to see the concern and worry in my eyes and face. Hear the care in my voice.

Sitting for a moment and then a quick headshake, "No! It is definitely Paul I am feeling."

"Then why wouldn't he take you to the back yard where you barbecued or to the basement to his weights. Or just in your bed in a dream; why, way out in the mountains," I asked, exasperated.

"Because they are mine. He told me years ago when we were there. He gave them to me in a flight of passion," with a sob. "So, I am going."

I put my hand gently on her shoulder.

"I still think tonight is too dangerous. And if something happens to you, how will I be able to prove Gregory did all this if you are not around to tell? Or if Paul does have something important to say, and you are killed by a bear or some equally frightening animal, how will anyone know?"

I paused to see if any of this was sinking in.

Apparently not.

"Wait until morning," I offered, "we will leave early, have coffee at the little café, and then you can continue up the trail from there, alone. It will be easier, safer, and I will feel much better about this entire event, please?"

Her shoulders dropped in an apparent weakening of defiance.

"If it is Gregory doing magicks, I will be nearby to help, even if it is just to call 911."

She seemed to relax, taking a moment to consider my proposition.

Finally, with a smile, "Maybe you are right. Paul will still be there in the morning. He wouldn't want me to get hurt. But we must leave at first light."

She made me promise.

The rest of the evening we spent empowering crystals in the closed circle. She knew most of the rite by rote. As we opened the circle, I was wearing two of the crystals and had several more in pockets and about my person. I was taking no chances. One of these stones might help protect me from magicks.

We turned in after another very subdued 'goodnight', with me still on the couch by mutual consent.

CHAPTER 17

I awoke to a distant noise, not sure what I was hearing - the garage door?

The alarms should be ringing, lights should be flashing and police should be driving up in droves with sirens, lights and guns drawn.

But, it was quiet. Too quiet.

Then I heard a car engine, which brought me wide-awake. I jumped from the couch and knocked on her bedroom door. With no answer, I opened it; saw the empty bed - and the note.

"Frankie, please do not follow. He needs me to come alone. I have to do this and have a last few thoughts with my Paul.

I do love you.

Jojo."

There was naught else to do but follow. I knew where she was going and I had to get there the quickest way. Throwing on hiking clothes and shoes, I picked my keys up from the ...

...they were gone.

She stole my keys!

Not wanting me to follow, she took my keys thinking to deter me. It would slow me for a moment, but that was about all. What she didn't know, I kept a spare set of keys in my trunk and a spare trunk key in my wallet. I have traveled extensively, and occasionally have lost or locked my keys in the car.

All the charged crystals went around my neck or into my pockets, a spare flashlight into my jacket and I was out the door.

I used my plastic key.

Driving as quickly as I could, I followed the earlier route, the one we took to spread Paul's ashes.

It was simple directions, *'right turn at the Bright Star Diner and straight on 'til...* well you know the way.

I didn't see her taillights. Either she pushed the speed envelope more than I was willing or there was a shortcut.

In retrospect, I should have known she would have slipped out while I slept. We were both fans of those old 'B movies'.

It happened all the same. The girl runs out, trying to do a deed on her own, against the better judgement of the hero. She becomes captive, gets beat up, and the hero goes through hell and back to save her.

After a very long ride with much recrimination, I arrived at the parking field. Moreover, after the verbal beating I gave myself, it surprised me I was still able to walk.

Jojo's car stood alone in the lot; therefore, maybe it was Paul sending the messages?

'NO!' I couldn't believe that. Gregory left his car somewhere else and magically teleported here.

I could feel him, a stickiness in the air. He was out there somewhere weaving spells.

I tested the flashlight, checked my pocket, and headed up the trail.

I had hid my approach as well as I could. My headlights were off when I neared the dark parking lot. Now I did the same with the flashlight, using it sporadically and keeping it shielded as I went along.

I followed her up the path.

And tailing her was easy. She had no shyness about calling out, or shining the light all around, and no reason to travel quietly. She called out to Paul several times.

How far would he bring her before making an appearance? And if it was him, I would head back to the car to await her return.

If it was Gregory, then I would have no choice but to do what I must to keep her safe. I am not big on violence, but if someone tries to hurt a loved one, then that person would be in for a rude awakening.

I do not play well with others who are trying to do me harm. Disabling someone just gives a second chance for them to get up and hurt you again. A man with a broken arm or leg can still kill you.

If he isn't breathing, he isn't killing. Most people who know me would not put me to the test.

I tried to keep near the side of the trail and quietly follow. Wandering passed the café, it was dark and deserted at this early hour. I kept one eye on the ground in front of me, and the other on her flashlight.

Unexpectedly, her light careened at a crazy angle. Did she slip, drop the flashlight? I moved forward to see what had happened.

Before I got more than a few steps…

"Who's there? Paul? Paul, is that you," she asked with a falter in her voice.

"*NO, BITCH.* Your idiot husband is dead and so will your friend be once my men get through with him. They should be breaking in about now. We wouldn't want him following us," he laughed maniacally.

It seemed that Gregory also spent far too much time watching 'B' movies on The Late Show.

I was beginning to lose my temper with this creep. I crept closer, looking for an opening. If I just ran headlong into the situation, he could hurt her. I didn't know what spells he had prepared. If I made the wrong move, alerted him to my being there, he could harm her just for spite.

The moon had risen, and the faint light cast an eerie glow.

I saw her try to call out, but her voice was as a whisper.

"Scream all you want. No one can hear. There is no one around for miles and I have be-spelled you to deaden sound."

Her face strained, she fought against him, tried to hold back her energy, to shield it from him. I didn't know how successful that would be.

I saw the tears streak her face.

Keep fighting Jojo.

I cheered her on silently, needing to get closer, formulate a plan. I wanted to surprise him, maybe separate them so I had a clear shot and not hurt her accidently. He had wrapped her wrists with tape to better confine her.

With arms immobilized, running would be difficult, and he could more easily keep her from fighting back.

But fight back she did.

He grunted and gasped a time or two as he warded from her fists and feet.

Good for you, Dear.

I was cautious, wanting to move silently up behind to take him down. But they were too close together and the darkness made it difficult to discern whom was who as they scuffled.

A few vines had entangled me, their tendrils ensnaring my legs, not wanting to let go. There had to be a spell on them. I pulled and twisted, freeing myself from some, then others would wrap around, enmeshing me again within their coils.

I watched the witch weave spells to get her guard down. But she resisted, fighting back. I saw the sweat glisten on her brow in the faint moonlight.

I lost my temper. The vine spell might hold animals but would not work long on me. My anger rose to the breaking point; my heart thumped wildly in my chest, my vision clouded. I reached up to wrench the vines that now encircled my throat, tightening about my neck.

I saw as the Warlock lost his temper. Frustrated that a mere woman could keep him from what he wanted.

"Bitch!" I heard as I saw him grab for her as she twisted, trying to get away. He reared back a fist.

I grabbed the last tendrils of vine, snatching them away from my face.

I yelled, *"NO! JOJO, WATCH OUT."*

She swung wildly; her arms flailed. Then amazingly Gregory flew across the glade, crumpling to the ground with a sickening thud.

The vines released me as she cried out.

In just a few steps, we were together. I shook, knowing how close I had come to losing her.

Tears streamed down her cheeks as I cut her bonds. Her arms locked around my neck in a strangle hold.

Her hug all but did the same.

"I'm sorry, I'm sorry," she whispered again, sobbing on my shoulder. "I should have listened to you."

I shushed her as we gingerly made our way to where the witch lay motionless. From the way he landed, I thought him dead.

Reaching my hand down to check for a pulse, I nearly fell as he disappeared, fading away to who knows where. I jumped back in shock. Jojo grabbed my arm to keep me from falling. We stood with mouths open as we watched him *POOF* out.

The revolver went back in my pocket.

Taking her by the shoulders, looking into her eyes, I asked, "Are you alright?"

With a tight smile, she nodded.

"Then let's get the hell out of here," I suggested.

We beat a hasty retreat to the parking lot, "we'll leave your car and come back for it later."

Another of my brilliant suggestions. I didn't trust her driving alone.

Hell, I wasn't sure about my own abilities right now. My hands still shook as the adrenalin tried to find an avenue through my system to burn off. I needed to concentrate while I safely navigated us home.

Funny, thinking of this as home.

Jojo relaxed and then more tears.

My free arm reached around and pulled her closer. "It's okay; it's over for now."

"Frankie, I was sure it was Paul," another gasping breath. "I was so sure."

"I know, I know. It's all right. You do not expect someone to do such a cruel thing, but he may have gotten a feel for Paul during the car crash. That was how Paul knew the Warlock was back."

"But how did you know it wasn't him," she inquired through the tears.

"He would never have brought you to a dangerous spot; he loved you too much. He would have just come to you in a dream."

My explanation was interrupted when …

"What the hell is that chirping noise?" Glancing to the dash for a clue, thinking maybe a car system was failing and then I checked the back seat.

Jojo's hand darted into her sweater, "It's my phone. I put it on vibrate because I didn't want the ringing to attract wild animals. Besides, I expected to get about twenty obscene phone calls from you," she laughed.

"I didn't take the time to call, being in too much of a hurry to come help a dear, dear friend," I mentioned. "Besides, I knew you wouldn't answer."

"I have six missed calls, all from the alarm company."

The phone rang again.

"Hello! Yes, this is she. What? No, we aren't home. The alarm activated and you notified the police. Good. They have two men in custody? We should be there in a few minutes. Yes, do that. Thanks, Bye," and she disconnected.

CHAPTER 18

She relayed, "The police had an extra patrol in our area; as they drove by the house, the alarms went off. They caught one man climbing in through the back window."

"We are going to have to trim or move those bushes; they offer to much cover," I explained.

"I would also like to know what happened to Gregory," I mused.

"He won't have any power left after all the spells. That last trick alone was an enormous drain." She paused to think for a moment how best to explain.

"It's an 'automatic'. Witches set up that spell to be activated when certain conditions are met, maybe uttering a phrase or in this case possibly unconsciousness, bringing him to a pre-arranged safe place."

Something caught her eye.

Reaching up, she felt one of the crystals dangling from my neck.

"Why are you wearing these," she asked.

"I thought I might need protection from Gregory. I have several of them."

She stretched to touch the other two I wore, "They are all dead, you know, burned out. These won't protect you."

"Impossible," I declared, "we just charged them. Reach into my pocket and pull out the pouch," I asked.

"No funny comments," as her hand roamed through my pocket. She pulled the pouch and emptied the stones into her palm.

"These are drained also. They are absolutely bereft of power, stone-cold dead."

"They shouldn't be, we charged them yesterday. I brought them all, wanting enough protection. He couldn't drain them while he was unconscious, could he," I queried.

"You weren't close enough. The power drained somewhere though."

"But, where," I quizzed.

"Let me think on that," she considered as we pulled up in front of the house.

"Wow! So many colored flashing lights here, it looks like a Christmas tree."

Five police cruisers idled.

Our friend, Sergeant Adams greeted us as we walked up. Jojo unlocked the front door and I slipped in to shut the alarm. Several officers followed on my heels, guns drawn; checking the house for more 'perps'. One stayed with me until the all clear came.

A circuit stayed lit, showing where the break-in occurred. He saw my consternation and explained the crew was still gathering evidence and they would secure the area when finished.

We walked towards the kitchen.

"Would you two look at the suspects," The Sergeant queried. "Maybe you know them, or they are familiar."

She gave him an odd stare.

"Sometimes we know the person or persons doing the crime. It does happen," he stated with authority.

The light in the back of the cruiser revealed the features of the men. They didn't look familiar to me. Jojo just stood there shaking her head, shivering from fear.

With a gloved hand, another officer brought a length of pipe to show that these men were here for more than simple robbery. Burglars travel light in the event they have to make a quick getaway.

"Did you find their car yet," I asked.

He shot me a quick complimentary nod.

"Well, they had to get here somehow. I do remember a few lessons from military police school," chuckling.

"I have two officers searching; one suspect had a car key in his pocket," the Sergeant said.

We had begun moving back to the house.

"Do either of you have enemies, someone wanting you hurt or dead," he questioned.

We reached the kitchen; I grabbed a Mountain Dew from the fridge for Jojo.

"You want coffee," I asked the Sergeant as I pointed to the pot.

He nodded, "We are waiting for Detective John Cleary to arrive. With the tools we found and the implements of mayhem, this became more than a simple burglary. We needed to turn the case over to the detective squad."

"Have a seat." I prompted.

I remembered one time we had visited Paul and Jojo; her little coffee pot nearly had a stroke from the strain. On one of my stops this trip, I saw a Bunn-o-matic brewer in the store. It makes delicious coffee in less than four minutes.

I looked across the table and she shrugged.

"Sarge," I began. "You know that old line, 'you wouldn't believe me if I told you?' That is what we have here. We do have someone after us, well, after Mrs. James and I guess he is now after me for interfering."

Sgt. Adams gave a funny stare. I rose to get the carafe as Jojo brought over the tray with the mugs and coffee fixings.

I looked at him as I filled his cup, "Do you know anything about the Para-normal?"

He thought for a moment, added sugar and sipped. "Good coffee," he commented, holding the cup up in a salute. "Maybe we'd best wait for the detective," and he settled deeper into the chair.

The forensic team had finished in the back room. "We taped plastic on the broken window," one man informed us. "The alarm is ready to be reactivated."

"Damn," Jojo cursed under her breath. "That is the second time this week that window has been broken," a slow head shake in frustration.

The alarm crew had replaced the previously broken one when they upgraded the system.

"We locked it, but it won't do more than keep out the draft," he smiled. They finished moving through the kitchen.

"Thanks guys," I said with a wave.

I had my cell phone out' texting the alarm company to order another window. At this rate, they may want to go into the business of replacing broken sashes.

I heard, "Yeah, Detective, in there," from the doorway. A man clad in a tan sport shirt and blue jeans walked in, an ID badge on his shirt pocket.

"Morning Bob," the detective greeted.

"Morning John," he returned in kind, "nice day! This is Mrs. James and Mr. Johnson. Folks, this is Detective John Cleary of our Violent Crime section."

We exchanged greetings as I poured more coffee, The Sergeant filled in the Detective on the goings on. His last sentence sat the detective back in his seat.

"They think it has to do with the Par-a-nor-mal," shaking his head as he said it.

The detective looked at both of us, opened a folder and proceeded to remove what turned out to be the neatly completed report on the break-in.

"Let's take care of what we can, first. I need signatures on the complaints to hold the 'perps'. You won't have to testify since the police caught them in the 'act of breaking and entering," he explained. "Then we can move on.

Jojo reached over and signed the paperwork.

He handed me the pen.

"I don't live here, so my signing has no meaning," I stated. He nodded, folded the report, and handed it to the Sergeant.

"You know where this needs to go, Bob. Thanks. I think I can handle it from here."

"No problem, John. I need to get out and see if they found the perps car. You folks 'be careful," He warned us; "if not, we'll be here."

We shook hands and he gave us a nice smile as he left.

"He would not have believed us, anyway," Jojo mentioned.

"What," I said.

"No feel for magick anywhere in him," was her reply. "There is an empty spot. I can sense …" as her head shook sadly.

Detective John watched our interplay, "Now tell me what is going on here."

I poured him the first of what would be many more cups of coffee.

We took turns telling the story, pouring more coffee and telling more of what we went through. Jojo got another Mountain Dew as we told him the last of what happened at the mountain.

"And you say these men worked for Gregory," Detective John asked.

"That is what I heard him tell Jojo. He hired them to keep me from following her," I replied.

"You heard him say that because you followed her to the mountains," he confirmed.

"Yes sir, that is correct. Gregory did not want me meddling in whatever he was doing. He sent his minions here to do me in."

"Then you said Mrs. James cold-cocked Gregory with her hands taped together," he repeated my statement with an incredulous look on his face.

"That is what it looked like from where I stood. I couldn't get close enough to do it, or I would have done more," I reported, remembering the rage I felt.

"I think I could have. Done it, I mean. I was twisting different ways, trying to get away, thinking he was going to hit me," she explained. "I was livid, not knowing Frankie was just feet away. Gregory had a spell on me that kept my senses from functioning properly. I thought Frankie was injured or ..."

"You walked over to check on Gregory, thinking you killed him. What happened next?"

"He just disappeared," Jojo said with a perfectly straight face.

"Yeah. He just kind of 'poofed' out," I concurred.

"POOFED'! Is that a technical term," he smiled.

"I think I read it in a sci-fi book about a wizard crow somewhere. It means to disappear by other than ordinary means or by Magicks," was my answer.

"Well, if you sign a complaint, we can look for him and bring him in. We can get him on possible kidnapping, assault and battery, battery with intent to commit mayhem; if his men finger him, possibly attempted murder."

He was already writing the report. He asked several pertinent questions, made a few remarks on the paper and it was ready for our signatures.

I gave it a quick read. He even managed to keep the Magicks out of it. I signed and handed the pen to Jojo, who also signed.

Taking a piece of equipment out of his case, he turned it on and ran the paper through it.

"This copies the form, then sends it digitally back to the precinct for the records; fast and easy; technology at its best," he quipped.

He cautioned us about taking matters into our own hands. "Vigilantes are frowned upon around here. It doesn't mean you can't defend yourself." He winked at that. "But I don't think we will find Gregory Rogers," he predicted. We both gave him a questioning look.

Detective John reached up and from his collar pulled a pendant similar to the one Jojo wore.

"I was part of a coven for many years, until I moved. I still keep in touch with everyone and participate when I get back home; which is why I didn't question your stories."

"Gregory Rogers is familiar to most groups. They exclude him. We don't mind if members dabble in a bit of dark arts, but this 'Warlock' does it exclusively, and for nefarious reasons. People die when he casts spells."

"He reportedly works with a politician who is gearing up for a run at the Presidency. The candidate has little chance, as it stands, to win. Only a miracle can get him the Oval office," the detective advised.

"Or black magicks, Detective," I ventured.

He glanced at me and smiled, nodding, "Call me John, please."

"We now know why he needs you so desperately, Jojo," I theorized. "With a big money client, he needs spells requiring massive power. I am not sure what spells would win an election," I finished.

"You can't make people vote for someone they don't want to vote for," she offered, "At least not in the numbers required in a large election. You would need to cloud the judgment of millions of people." She stood there looking at both of us.

"Let me check with a few folks I know. Perhaps I can come up with the answer," he offered. "In the meantime, we will continue the extra patrols in the neighborhood."

We shook hands,

"Thanks John."

Jojo reached her hand out; he took it and smiled, feeling the power in her. He bowed his head in respect. "Blessed Be, dear Lady."

She blushed slightly, "Blessed Be!" And showed him to the door.

Sitting back down, I took a sip of coffee.

"I think I need a nap," she sighed, "and a shower," as she walked back into the room.

"Yes, me too. I thought once I reached a certain age I would be able to sleep in once in a while," I joked.

She sat across the table from me, appearing nervous. Her eyes darted back and forth, then went to the stones which she held in her hands, looking deeply into them.

"What are you doing," I wondered.

"Recharging the crystals, we may need them and I don't want to run short."

CHAPTER 19

Rising, I picked up the empty mugs, placed the soda bottles in the recycle bin and proceeded to wash the cups and silverware. After several minutes of silent chores, we were both done. Now I was very ready for that shower and nap.

I gathered my toiletries and headed for the guest bathroom. I heard her shower go on a few moments earlier.

The one attribute I remembered Paul telling me about the bathrooms, they had their own water heaters and the shower valves were thermostat driven. You set the water to the temperature you wanted and they maintained that temperature. So I had no qualms about using all the hot water I wanted. The system was cheap and efficient. The shower was of a goodly size, and set up for steam. He said after a hard workout, the steam was what he needed most.

The hot water cascaded down my body, it was thoroughly enjoyable as it relaxed my muscles. The steam worked its way into my head and sinuses and cleared everything away. I closed my eyes, the rhythm of the water lulled me; the stress rinsed down the drain with the water; just drifting and then...

I was not alone.

I sensed someone.

The steam was thick. I was startled to feel two hands on my shoulders; soft, light, caressing. They reached around, entrapped me as I felt hot breath at my ear, hands worked, caressing my chest. Lips nuzzled my neck as her body brushed against mine.

"Frankie, I was so scared out there," with a whispered sob, "For both of us. I thought I might never see you again; that you may have been killed."

Her voice broke. "I didn't know that I could feel that much sorrow losing someone. It didn't hurt that bad when Paul died. But when that witch said he sent men to kill you, I lost my mind."

"He reared back to punch me. I wanted to fight him with everything I had."

She paused, her senses over-whelmed. "I couldn't, I had no energy, no power. I was weak as a kitten. Then he swung, I cowered and - he was flying through the air," a gasp at the memory.

I turned towards her while she spoke. I held her; caressed her. She ceased talking as our lips met.

That kiss was more intense, more intimate, and more sensual than before. I nearly drowned in it, and it had nothing to do with the water. She took my hand, led me from the bathroom, down the stairs and into her bed. We lay to catch our breaths.

I rolled onto my side to let my hand trail the contours of her breast, allowing my finger to run circles around her already aroused nipple. My mouth found hers; again, our tongues dueled for supremacy. No care who won, both or none. I bit lightly her lip and pulled back to look deeply into those pretty blue eyes.

I searched for a certain glimmer there, an assuredness in her demeanor. I didn't want to mix my signals and do something she suddenly didn't feel ready to do. The smile I saw gave me the confidence that this was the proper thing, the right thing.

My mouth went back down, crushing her lips. Our tongues again imbibed in that sensual interchange of passion. Mine stopped, moved off, trailed down her neck, little stabs eagerly tasted along the way, elicited the low moan from her pouty lips.

My hand traced another line down her slightly rounded belly; Goosebumps rose as it tickled spots along her thigh. My tongue paused at the aureole already puckered in anticipation. It danced there a moment. A slight cry and moan from somewhere.

Her hand lightly brushed across my chest, softly played on my nipple, caused my skin, and more, to respond.

Her other hand on the back of my neck, guided as I suckled. She shivered. The hand became more insistent crushing my mouth against her skin.

Her thighs, hot in anticipation parted as I moved.

A deep sigh escaped me. The vibration around her nipple caused her to whimper.

Another moan as I moved again. My lips back on hers as my knees found purchase on the mattress. A feeling of 'oneness', of completion overcame me as I found a steady rhythm pleasing to us both.

I saw the look in her eyes turn to wonder as a drop of water fell to her chest. She reached up to my face and her fingers came away wet.

I was crying and didn't realize it.

And then tears brimmed her eyes.

The feelings changed to expectancy as the tempo quickened. What was once a slow cadence, now moved to a quick march. An urgency overtook our senses. My lips back down upon hers. A cry from somewhere; a shudder as her legs enwrapped my hips, clamped, then relaxed, then back to clenching harder.

She ground up against me, her arms about my neck, mine around her back. I pulled up, bringing her with me. Only my knees upon the bed.

Once more we moved together, bound together in each other. Sobs and tremors ran through our bodies, until finally, with one last small shudder. I lay her back upon the bed. Our lips still locked in contented completion.

"I meant what I wrote," she sighed again. "In the note, that last part. I wasn't entirely sure at the time," she admitted. "Oh! I knew there were feelings roiling, but I wasn't sure until he said he was having you killed."

"Then I knew. If something happened to you, I couldn't go on." She began to sniffle quietly.

I softly rubbed her thigh as I rolled away, up on one elbow. She looked up at me and smiled.

We fell into each other's arms again.

I shushed her, "Don't talk, we'll talk later," I assured her. "It's all right, it's okay." I kissed each of her eyes, then the tip of her nose. I reached over to kiss her beautiful lips, she hesitated, and then we nearly got lost in each other, again. We tasted in each other the expectations of the future.

My hand roamed down her thigh, caressed, pinched, and slapped lightly. As we rolled over, my mouth fell to her nipple, and I again suckled. Her hand went down between my legs where I was becoming; rising to the occasion, alive again, much to my satisfaction and hopefully hers.

She gave a squeeze and then squealed as I playfully bit her nipple in retaliation. She started to roll onto her back. I stopped her and we rolled the other way.

"It is much better this way with you on top. Besides, you are lighter."

Her legs straddled my thighs, we played for position. I caressed her magnificent breasts as they swayed above me, catching an occasional nipple in my teeth, and then trying for a mouthful of the other one. Her hips did a slow dance, trying to capture me. I played, watching her; the slight smile; the concentration, then straining at some fast passing emotion as she enjoyed a small orgasm here and then there.

Her pretty face, never still, a myriad of expressions forever captured my heart; her beautiful blue eyes, the iris swelled, narrowed as her soft blond hair obscured her vision briefly.

Suddenly my heart nearly burst; I realized that I have loved her all my life and never knew it. All right, I knew, but was afraid to admit it. Now, through tragic events, I had everything I had ever wanted, right here.

Down below, I let her win that battle. I went willingly as a prisoner. Incarcerated in that womanly jail for a sentence that I wanted to last a lifetime and tried to endure as long as humanly possible.

We screamed and moaned, shuddered together for long moments that lasted forever, finished entirely too soon. Climbed, rose, almost... no!

A slap lightly on her ass cheek, my finger headed for a rear assault. She bent, kissed me hard, her tongue played within me, her hand sneaked up to twist my nipple. I moaned, bit her lip; she was there, I was right behind; we screamed into each other. Our senses over-loaded, glans expanded, exploded; floating forever and a day. She froze, I couldn't move, time stood still.

I lost that battle.

She looked at me with tears in her eyes; collapsed atop me. My knees rose, trapping her.

My arms embraced her tightly; never wanting to move again.

Contentedness overwhelming, I knew I lost the battle, but won the war.

We both sighed as she nuzzled my ear.

"No!" I whimpered.

"No?"

"No! Nothing left, drained, empty." I whispered tiredly.

"Me too," she giggled.

"Happy, content, ecstatic," I smiled.

"Me too," giggling again.

And then, "We have a slight problem."

I looked at her, startled.

"One of us needs to go shut the water in the shower."

"We never turned it off, did we," I laughed.

"No, we became involved in what we were doing like two high school lovers in a hurry before getting caught."

She giggled again. "I remember hearing it as the shower door closed."

I groaned, "I'll go."

She rolled off me with a groan of her own and smiled, "that was fun, that way. You were right though, I'm impressed," commenting with a nod to the alarm clock, "two hours, nearly."

Leaning over, I got a quick kiss on my lips as I moved off the bed.

"For me, at my age, that is all day," I quipped.

Padding out of the bedroom and up the stairs, strangely I didn't hear anything. The sounds of the water cascading in the shower that should have assailed my senses were quiet.

There was nothing to see, either. Steam that should have filled the hallway was absent. I investigated further.

The water was off and had been for a while as seen by the dryness of the floor. I tried different scenarios attempting to turn the faucets.

Only physically turning the knobs and handles shut the water.

I pondered the question while I took care of certain needs and washed up before returning to the bedroom.

Jojo had had the same idea in her bathroom and was stretched back out on the bed.

"How much water needed to be wiped up," she asked with concern.

"None," I replied. "It was off, and judging by how dry the shower was, it had been off for quite some time." I sat and took her hand.

"Let me think on it a while," she mused.

"Slide over while you give it thought then, I more than ever need that nap, now."

She slid without argument and I stretched out next to her.

Rolling onto my side, facing her, I propped my head on my hand.

"Dear Lady; it is my realization that I am and have always been deeply in love with you. Looking up at you a while ago, the tears formed in my eyes as you smiled. Then I knew this is where I am supposed to be, and what I am supposed to be doing," I whispered.

"Doing what," she whispered in expectation.

"Making you happy," I said in all seriousness.

I pulled her head to me and gave her a soulful kiss. Pulling back slightly, her head shifted as if to get a better look at me and she smiled.

"Are you sure, Frankie," she asked guiltily, with hope in her voice.

"Entirely! Though you will have to take my word for it, for now." I leaned in and gave another touch of my lips on hers.

"It really is nap time. These old bones need at least an hour or two."

I settled down; watched as she set the alarm on the phone; turned back to me and snuggled up.

We both slept peacefully.

CHAPTER 20

I opened my eyes, reached over to shut the phone alarm, and then did a double take as the phone didn't look familiar. Neither did the room for that matter. Where did Judy and I get to that put us in this unknown bedroom? We traveled a lot, but I always knew where ...

I began to rise; felt the warmth of the body next to me, smiled as memories came flooding back and then felt empty.

For a moment, I was back in time. I looked over at Jojo, asleep peacefully, as I remembered Judy.

I sighed, shook my head. It's all right to feel sad, but I needed to hold back on the emotions for now, time enough later to drop into depression.

Events were going to get rather strange and I wanted to give Jojo some peace. I softly padded back upstairs to my bathroom.

By the time I finished, it was with a new mindset. The shower was hot and soothing; the steam was relaxing. The future was out there; I was with the woman I loved dearly, and *all was good with the world*!

Well! Except for that demon who would be searching for me, a warlock who wanted to enslave Jojo, kill me and help rule the world. But it wasn't too terrible. A few minor hurdles to get over and we could start a new and happy life.

I thought, maybe a nice omelet.

I chopped a green onion, a bell pepper, added a few bean sprouts and made fresh coffee. Almost everything was ready when I heard the whistle from the hall.

"Don't you wear clothes when you cook," I saw her leering. She was wearing a short little nightie that was sexier than if she had been nude.

"Well, to tell you the truth, No! My famous quote is, 'look how much money you can save on laundry if you never wear clothes," I teased. "But you may have something, with Gregory running around loose I should wear some covering; just in case." I slid the omelets onto the platter, placed it on the table, "I'll be right back."

In a moment, I returned wearing a pair of shorts.

"However, once that witch is history, the shorts are too. I love the feeling of freedom it gives me." I winked at her as I speared more egg.

We sat and ate; we discussed and made plans.

Most important, we talked.

"Look," I said, as I took her hand. "This is going to be difficult."

Pulling her hand away in anger and sliding further back in the seat, she glared at me; arms crossed, "Well, go ahead."

For a minute, I sat, stunned, not sure what I did. Then it struck me; what thoughts must be running through her head.

"No, that is not what we need to discuss. I am sorry if you thought I would do that to you; after doing that to you."

"I am sincere in what I said and no second thoughts."

I reached for her hand. A slight hesitation and it went back in mine.

"We are going to have some hard times ahead; not financially. Judy and I had insurance on each other and the royalties from the book should be good, along with the latest WIP (*work in progress*)."

I paused to get my emotions in check. "We are going to have many feelings in the next few weeks while we get used to new situations." I swallowed as I thought of my next words.

"Earlier, I awoke not knowing where I was. The surroundings looked unfamiliar. I thought Judy and I had spent the night in a strange hotel room." I choked up, with the memories of my wife, her smile, and I sighed. "That is what I mean. You go through it too, I've noticed."

She gaped as if I had discovered a deep, dark secret about her; and surprised that I had even noticed.

"It's okay," I reassured squeezing her hand. "We went through many years; good and bad with them. They deserve our remembrances, our sorrow, and our tears. It's okay to cry, to get mad and throw something because your husband was murdered."

"I will never feel jealous of Paul because you remember him."

I dropped my head and a tear ran down my cheek, remembering Judy.

With a pat on my hand, "I noticed a few times," she soothed, "when you had that faraway look in your eye; and you stood, unmoving. I wondered what long ago scene you were recollecting with her? I worried that your love for me won't be entirely for me, but transference from her." She frowned a moment and shook her head.

"But…" I began to explain.

"No!" Her finger on my lips, which I kissed lightly, stilled my voice as she continued, "I know you love me. Just about two days I sat here after Paul died, waiting for you. I re-read some of your writings. I had saved them on line and in e-mails. All of your poems dealing with relationships and love, they were written with me in mind. I see dates on them; some from when we were together. However, the others are later, but still written the same. Even though you may have put another's name to it, you were thinking of me, all these years." She paused, a tear forming.

I nodded, "Yes! I loved my spouses deeply, never cheating on them; I was faithful as a husband could be. But a little corner of my mind, and a little piece of my heart I kept for you."

I continued softly, "All those years apart, I looked for you, asked about you; but no one would tell me where you were, how you were. I hadn't known your married name, but I looked, anyway. When the internet came out, I searched. Do you know how many Joanna's are listed in phone books," I joked.

"And of the poetry, you are right. It was written with you in mind, nearly all of it," I whispered.

"B-but, why," she looked puzzled.

"You were the inspiration; you were the catalyst that opened the floodgates to my emotions; my creativity; my sensitivity. You were my Muse. Without us corresponding those forty years ago, there would be no writing. We loved each other and then it ended. We walked away. I didn't want to. I loved you so much it hurt."

I shook my head slowly before continuing. "But, you said you didn't know, you weren't sure and I wanted what you thought would make you happy. So, I walked away."

A few more tears fell, and not just mine.

She gave my hand another shake and let go. Then stood, looking down at me.

I thought she was going to ask me to leave; bringing back too many old memories.

"Frankie, let me explain," a whisper as tears ran down her cheeks. "I loved you, really." A momentary pause, a slight smile passed across her lips as if she remembered a long ago time.

"I was drowning in it; getting lost in our love. All the plans, I was afraid, scared that it would all crumble and fall to dust. I had been brought up to be a failure. Nothing I did was ever right." She stopped to take a breath, to get thoughts in order.

"You began to show me that it wasn't true; that I had worth. You saw characteristics in me that I hadn't known were there; traits no one else saw. You reminded me, believed in me. But I panicked," disengaging our hands, she paced.

"I listened to the horror stories of my relatives and their miserable marriages and how all their unions fell apart. They said it was in our blood. I didn't want that for us. I was young back then, and not so smart."

She walked over and retrieved another bottle of pop from the icebox; returned to sit, leaning on the table.

"I wanted you to be happy. If my first marriages were doomed from the start, as my relatives said, I should be the one to hurt, not you."

She stopped to chuckle, "You saw how our siblings' marriage worked out."

"So, not to hurt me, you hurt me," I queried.

"I thought a few weeks of misery would be all, and then you would be over me," she explained. "I didn't realize ..."

I sat for a few moments, taking it all in. "I can't fault you for your sentiment. Though, if we had just talked about it; we might have worked it out," I reasoned.

"Well, we both went through several marriages," she reminded me.

"Yes, but to other people. We might be celebrating a forty-something anniversary with each other."

I squeezed her hand and smiled. "It's alright. I just wanted to clear the air so we both understood that we could relive the past for a bit. It is what we are. Pleasant memories from times past can help relieve the stress of today."

I paused for a breath. "We are going to feel guilt. There is no cure for it, but time. Give in to it occasionally. Wallow in it if you want, for a few minutes. Then come back here, to me, to the present. The same with self-pity; it is okay to do it… for a little while."

"At times yelling and screaming about the atrocities in our lives, our pasts, can help us to get over it, to work through it. But limit that time."

I reached out my other hand, to have both her hands in mine. I looked deeply into her very pretty eyes, sighed, wanting to get lost in them.

"I just want you to know that I love you. Whatever time we have left, I will be here, ALWAYS…"

A quick nod as she attempted to speak, to try to breathe. A long sigh escaped her lips.

"I know," she whispered.

We sat contented for a time, staring at each other, just holding hands; no thoughts about tomorrow.

She cleared her throat, "I think we had better get busy; it's getting late."

We let go of each other, somewhat reluctantly.

"I don't think Gregory will have sufficient power to try any attack until tomorrow. Until he can recharge, we will be safe," she assured me.

"Maybe we should go get something to eat." I suggested. She liked that idea.

As in any emotional situation, sometimes we forget the little niceties in life, the creature comforts, and the 'not-so-important things – like food.

We dressed, set the alarm system and walked out to the car.

CHAPTER 21

Our favorite waitress Janet had the night off so we met Sue. Pleasant, courteous, efficient, and quiet, which is just what we needed. Though, I think *'in awe'* would be more of an accurate description.

Sue hemmed, hawed, and fawned over us. She knew who we were and what had befallen us, as did most people in the diner, by now.

Our being there elicited everything from sly glimpses to outright stares, to one little girl who pointed and exclaimed in a loud voice, *"Look, Mommy, the witch people."*

I thought to sit near them and cackle, to make their night memorable.

Jojo took my hand, smiled to the little girl, and thought that was good enough.

'Spoilsport ...'

We took it all in stride.

As we finished our salads, I pointed out a familiar figure; Detective John Cleary stopped at the counter, exchanged a few words with the waiter and pointed towards the rear of the diner. Seeing us, holding up an index finger, he again pointed to the men's room.

I nodded.

Jojo looked at me and shrugged.

A few moments later, he was back, wiping his hands on the cheap paper towels they used in every restroom.

"Fancy meeting you here," he quipped. "I was going to call you in the morning. I think we found the 'perp' who tried to break-in that first time."

She looked askance, "I thought Gregory attempted the first robbery?"

No," John corrected, sitting down next to me in the booth, "Gregory does none of the menial tasks. He hires out for that."

"So, you don't think the same people did both attempts," I asked.

"No, different MO," he explained. "That first night was just a test of your alarm system; quiet, simple, to see how best to get in. Even if you were home that night, you would not have heard anything. That man had the trait of being neat and precise."

"The second break-in was a smash and grab, in and out. Do the deed; make it appear a robbery gone sour where they kill the target to get away."

"Did this other guy work for Gregory, did you question him," she prodded.

"Well," he hesitated a moment, "No, We found him in an abandoned warehouse, naked on an inverted Pentagram. His arms and legs nailed to the floor, his heart sliced out, and by the look of the pained and surprised expression on his face, he was alive and awake as it all happened.

Sue chose that moment to bring our dinner. Steaks, medium, mashed potatoes with gravy.

I smiled at John; Jojo blanched; I chuckled and shrugged.

And then he realized we had not eaten, "I am so sorry," he apologized.

Jojo gave a weak smile, rose, and a weaker, "Excuse me," squeaked out.

He again apologized. "Sometimes I get involved and forget where and to whom I am speaking. Sorry about being graphic."

I had Sue bring his coffee and pie to the table.

"Have you eaten yet," I offered.

He nodded. "This is just a snack to tide me over."

"I think it will be all right," I began. "With all she has gone through this past week, her husband gone just a few days, and Gregory out there, it has been hard. It bothers me to think of all the hurt this beautiful lady…"

A hand caressed my shoulder. I slowly tilted my head back. She stared down at me, a sad smile across her lips.

Bending to kiss me, "Once more, my white knight defending me against the evil forces of everyday life," she quipped.

John stood, "Again, I'm sorry." He apologized a third time.

She motioned him to sit.

"It's okay, John. Little sleep, long days, emotional stress. Normally, graphic talk does not bother me. Tonight it just hit the senses wrong."

She looked down at her plate, took a forkful of mashed potato, then back up at him shyly. "I see that 'detective look'. Yes, I did just bury my husband of twenty-four years. It does look peculiar, me kissing Frankie that way. However, we planned a wedding some forty years ago. We both went through the trauma of losing spouses. Frankie's wife died about a week ago."

She continued, "When we reconnected on the internet a few years back, we realized the forty years never happened. For us, it was the 1970's again. Our problem …" Jojo stopped to get her emotions under control.

I reached a hand across the table for her to hold.

"…we were still very much in love with our spouses. Frankie and Judy lived on the East Coast. For vacations, the four of us met and had great fun. We all got along."

"I have helped him on a few of his books. He and Paul had similar interests, while Judy and I lurked through the dark and out-of-the-way shops hunting hidden treasures." She stopped to spear another piece of steak.

I picked up the telling, "John, my wife died tragically of fright. An entity invaded our home and scared her to death."

I took a breath, "and I think it's still there."

He gave me one of those, 'you have got to be kidding' detective looks.

"The police and EMT's trying to revive Judy raced from the house with her as the entity threw furniture; slammed doors and utterly terrified them."

He gave me a quizzical look.

"It attacked one night, luring me to the backyard, throwing deck chairs, a picnic table. Then it locked me out, trapping my wife in. I called 911 for help and finally managed to break a sliding glass door to get back to her. The emergency services warned me to never call them again."

"Where did the entity come from," he wanted to know.

"Judy, with a few of her friends brought it through on an Ouija board. I warned them of the consequences if they used it without proper safe guards. They thought it was fun. Eventually they connected with the wrong spirit. I tried telling her to dispose of the board."

"I found it in a closet right before the attacks began. We did burn it after closing the gateway, but it was too late."

He gave me another curious look.

"We had the house blessed, well partially; the priest ran from our bedroom after the entity told him where to put the lit candle the altar boy was holding." I took a sip of coffee.

"A psychic barely made it through the front door. She ran, screaming, clutching at her head in panic. I think she is still screaming," I chuckled.

"I know; it is not truly funny. Nevertheless, we have been through experiences most people wouldn't believe could happen in a science fiction or horror story. But we have lived it. So, it doesn't seem terrible to us, to enjoy life, whatever time we have left, and the hell with what the rest of the world thinks as propriety."

Sue had brought more coffee. John was on his second piece of cheesecake.

"Very nutritious," Jojo joked.

"I eat healthy at home, but when I get the chance to splurge once in a while; as you said, 'Life is too short!'"

He gave her another strange glance, and then offered, "allow me give you a card of someone who may be able to help you."

Handing it over to her, a strange, perplexed look flashed on his face as she took it from his hand.

Jojo read, *"The Candle Shoppe. Custom candles, Wicca supplies, 'stop in and we will 'bewitch' you shortly. Joseph and Kyra Athame, proprietors."*

"We have met them. Nice couple. Frankie thinks Kyra is a 'pussycat'," she smirked.

"Oh, she is; one of the gentlest creatures on earth, but if you cross her, the claws come out," he smiled.

"I got this Crystal from him," she pulled the stone from under her blouse for John to look at.

He stopped and stared. "Is that what I was feeling?"

Sitting up, more at attention, he wanted to touch it, looked almost afraid, in awe. I watched as his hands nearly caressed it, but then he pulled away. Just a glimpse was enough to affect him emotionally.

"I have heard much about that stone, but never thought in all my life I would ever get a chance to see it. We've heard rumors of where it was."

"Did Joseph tell you about this stone," he asked.

"He said a little, how it knows whom to help and when to leave; but not much else," she replied.

"Just like him to downplay the importance of such a … That stone is so rare, and the power, WOW."

Watching him look around as he spoke, he appeared almost afraid that someone would overhear.

"No one knows from whence it came, but legend has it; it belonged to *MERLIN the MAGICIAN.*"

I gaped at him, "Oh, come on, John. Are we supposed to believe that that is a magickal stone from a mythical person from the past?"

He looked at me and solemnly nodded.

"They claim the Magick, which was *MERLIN*, was placed in that stone by the Magician himself upon his death. That stone is so precious. One auction house in London appraised it at 'over three million pounds', more than twelve million dollars, American. And that was mid-1800."

He stopped to sip coffee and get his nerves under control. It excited him, so I didn't think he was lying.

"Don't show that to anyone else," he cautioned.

"The story goes, back in 1896; the Crystal was up for sale. The Auction house entrusted it to a museum to keep it safely in their vault. Twenty trusted British Advisors and experts watched it locked away."

"That same group retrieved it the next day, plus the guards. As the curator reached to remove it from its container, an eerie blue light pulsed, temporarily disorienting them. When they regained their senses, the Stone had vanished."

"But they remembered the eerie laughter afterwards. All in the vault were strip-searched, with nothing resolved."

His coffee cup shook slightly as he took a sip.

"That was the last time that it reportedly appeared. Stories spread throughout the covens over the years; where it was, whom did it help; speculation as to where next it would show up."

"Just know that it is a very powerful ally, and when you are safe; the work done; it will move on."

He rose to leave, reaching for the check Sue had brought; I grabbed it first. With much protesting, he finally allowed me the honor.

"For all the help and information, at least we can buy a friend a coffee," I said. "We'll even pass on your greeting to Joseph and Kyra."

We shook hands and he left.

Jojo sat there, her hand on her blouse over where the crystal lay.

"I felt that it was powerful, but not that powerful," looking up at me, "and valuable like that? I never would have guessed; and *MERLIN*?"

Sue came back to see if all was well, concerned that John was questioning us.

"No, he is just a friend," I related to her.

"Oh," she sighed, "That explains it, then."

"Explains what, Sue?" Jojo asked, now taking an interest in the conversation.

"Why he paid your bill when he paid his," she said with a smile.

I held the two receipts out to her.

"He used the 'dupe' copies. He did say that you should take care of the tip though, and to be nice to me," she giggled.

I mimicked my best Cagney impression,

"That dirty rat."

I looked down at the cash in my hand, removed smaller denominations, and handed her the remaining bills, including the twenty.

Sue looked at the cash, back to me, "I hope you have more friends to meet at the diner. Thanks," and walked away, smiling.

CHAPTER 22

We didn't know if the Candle Shoppe would still be open. It wasn't late for us, *nine pm* and the night was just starting. To a business, though, it was mostly closing time. The lights still blazed, so we parked the car and walked up to the entrance, not knowing if they could truly help.

They acted as if they knew we would be visiting.

"Good evening and 'Blessed Be", Kyra greeted with a smile. "Joseph is in the back and will be right out. Have a seat," she offered, pointing to the conversation area we used previously. "I need to lock the front door."

"You're closing," I asked. "We could come back tomorrow."

"Nonsense; sit, we'd consider it an honor," she assured us.

A disembodied voice came from behind the curtain. Joseph pushed his way through carrying a tray of mugs, bottles, and cookies.

"We were waiting for you!"

He pointed to the mug with coffee, and we helped ourselves to cookies.

I watched Kyra pick up her mug. She looked at me, smiling as she sipped.

"What," questioning my stare.

Jojo jumped in, "he was expecting you to be sipping a saucer of cream, I think."

She smiled at that. "I have that before curling up on my bed," she joked, blinked twice, and went back to her tea.

Joseph looked at us, eyes narrowing, gauging. "Something's changed!"

We looked to each other and smiled sheepishly. Jojo answered, "Yes, we decided that life was too short to mourn our spouses. We will always miss them and love them, but we have to move on. We will be with them in the unfolding."

"That was not to what I referred."

He looked at me. "Have you gone through a catharsis, something momentous?"

I smiled and...

"No," he said, holding up his hand, palm towards me. "I am not referring to a few hours of wild love-making," he smirked, shook his head. "I've got to get that fixed."

We three broke up laughing.

"What," looking back to us.

I sipped my coffee, "In all seriousness, though," I told him, "Yes, when I saw Gregory try to harm Jojo, it slammed into my head that I was absolutely and hopelessly in love with her."

I reached over without even thinking about it and took her hand.

"I was fearful that she would be hurt; it infuriated me."

"What happened?"

I explained about the spell, how she headed into the mountains. I told him the events that led up to where Gregory said he had minions out after me, to kill me. "And then, Jojo somehow knocked him out before I could even get there, as I was caught in those damnable vines. She swung, hit him and he flew eight feet."

"Is he captured or dead," was the anxious question.

"Neither," Jojo interjected. "He vanished; he had a 'spell of recall.'"

Both he and Kyra nodded, "Common spell for someone of his ilk," she commented, looking towards her husband.

"How did you feel right before you struck him," he asked.

"Tired; weak; drained; funny thing, Frankie's crystals had drained and he wasn't near the witch," she finished.

Kyra cleared her throat, looking to him, "I don't think…" She began to say when he cut her off.

"No, I don't think we should say anything yet."

"But…" Kyra began again.

"No!" He said politely but firmly. "I don't feel the time is right."

"What," Jojo asked. "Is there something you are afraid to tell us; something about one of us?"

"Not afraid to tell," he started and stopped.

"You feel, um, uncomfortable," I probed.

"I believe it is not the proper time to talk about this, is all," he declared

"Can you tell us if it is life threatening," I wondered. "I'm not going to walk out the door and be run over by a bus or something, am I?"

"The bus doesn't come down this street," he kidded back. And then seriously, "No, not life threatening," he answered with a shake of his head and a confirmed look to Kyra.

She sat, shook her head along with him.

"Significant, perhaps, but not life threatening," she intoned.

"Then don't tell us," I stated plainly.

Jojo looked horrified, as if having an unopened Christmas gift pulled away.

Kyra looked stunned also.

Joseph sat back, more relaxed, the tension faded from the room. "Are you sure?"

"Yeah, if it is not dangerous, not life threatening, I'll wait." I looked to Jojo, who sat with a worried stare.

"You should look worried," I told her. "He is more likely to say I am going to be a father again. That would be 'momentous', at my age, I am sure." I kidded her to lighten the mood.

She blushed, "That wouldn't be momentous, it would be more along the lines of 'miraculous', since I can't conceive babies anymore, no matter how many times we try," she giggled.

As we settled down, Joseph said, "You want to know about spells and protections."

Jojo looked at me and we shrugged, not ever having voiced that request, yet.

"Yes, that witch got to Jojo much too easily, luring her into the mountains. Now, we believe he will make a full frontal assault, and we need something to protect her from him."

"He also sent two thugs to the house that night to kill Frankie," she interjected. "He wasn't at home because he was out saving me."

I saw Joseph nod to Kyra at that last statement.

"There is not much in the way of help we can give," he began to say. "The basic premise of our belief is, *'IF IT HARMS NONE, DO WHAT YOU WILL."*

He sat, watching our reaction and continued.

"You see, we are in a bit of a quandary. We want to help, to avoid you coming to harm, but as for offensive spells, we could give you very little. Gregory runs under no such compunction as a black witch. Just know, if he throws a spell at you, the crystals will protect you. You will be safe. There are unseen forces that will see that you survive," He advised.

"Yes, we know, thank you," Jojo began."

They both sat up to listen.

"We met an old friend of yours; John Cleary. He filled us in on the crystal you loaned me."

"John, sure! We have known him for years. He was always into the rumors and superstitions," Joseph said, smiling with a quick glance at his wife.

"But, again, there is not much in the way of spells we can give to you. Even regular spells need planning, working through, and preparing for."

"It is not like the movies, where they pull a wand, say a few 'Magick words' and people turn into frogs. That is just in fantasy. Here it takes much time and energy to set up spells," he educated.

"Joseph is right," his wife agreed, "we don't want to see you hurt, but witchcraft in real life is not as depicted on the TV or in the movies. Needless to say, 'Bewitched' is not our favorite TV show, and Harry Potter ..." she shook her head with a wan smile. "Witchcraft is a serious avocation. But when the time comes, what you will need and the power to do it will be there; and from more than just that stone."

"If you need help with the other problem, Kyra should be able to assist," Joseph said cryptically.

We had finished our beverages and had eaten most of the cookies. We felt relaxed, refreshed, as if just awakened from a great nap.

Kyra, while collecting the mugs and dishes reached out to touch my shoulder. I felt the shock run through me, looked down to see if the shirt burned or the skin singed but there was not a mark on me.

She smiled pleasantly, *"Mote It Be!"*

Joseph walked us to the door, stopped a moment; reached to shake my hand.

As our fingers met, a spark jumped from me to him. He flinched in surprise.

"First; I feel that Kyra gave you her Special Blessing."

"Is that what that was," I asked.

"Second," he continued, nodding, "when the warlock shows, once he feels the energy, he will not stay long. Other forces are gathering and you both will walk out the other side. He will not bother you for a goodly time, if ever after."

"Blessed Be, my friends," he said sincerely.

"Blessed Be," we replied in kind.

Walking to the car, "We never asked him half the questions we needed to know," I mentioned to Jojo.

"No," she chuckled, as I held the car door for her, "But, somehow I think he answered them."

CHAPTER 23

It was an uneventful ride home, nothing attacked, and nothing broke through the windows. I pulled up in the driveway and grabbed a nine iron from the golf bag in the trunk.

There had been ideas of me taking up the game, but just not the time. I pictured Judy and me tooling around the country, and my playing at courses; walking the fairways and greens made famous by the likes of Snead, Jones, Woods and Mickelson. Someday maybe, so, I kept the clubs.

The joke made by one of my sons; instead of getting me a golf cart, they would get me a camel or a submarine. I think I wrote that child out of my will.

With iron in hand, I made a circuitous tour of the outside; everything seemed in order. We unlocked the door, checked and recycled the alarm. All was quiet as we settled. Possibilities needed discussions, where do we live, do we marry. Ideas had to be kicked around.

Then the silly line came to mind; funny how that happens when you are expecting a warlock to jump out and kill you, about *'planning your wedding for early in the morning, so, if it doesn't work out, you still have time to get a date for the reception.'*

I chuckled at my own joke.

Jojo had gone to get comfortable. The coffee brewer dripped, and I was about to ask if she wanted a 'dew' when I noticed the icebox door was open. Not fully open, but just a little ajar. I checked and all was right, the freezer had everything still frozen. It could not have been open long.

"Do you want a soda?"

"Yes, Dear," came the reply.

I placed the bottle on the table, turned the cap to loosen and poured my coffee. I retrieved a glass for her and sat, awaiting her return.

A sigh came from over my right shoulder and my quick thought; she had snuck in to surprise me. I turned to see … no one.

With a shrug I continued to sip my coffee.

A few moments later, she padded in, clad in a short robe, slid her arms around my neck and kissed me.

"What was that for," I asked with a contented smile.

"Because I love you, and because I can," she answered with a smile of her own. She sat opposite and poured her drink.

"A strange happenstance. I went to get your soda from the icebox and the door was ajar. Nothing ruined or out of place, but it definitely stood open. Something doesn't feel right," I mentioned. "And just before you came in, I heard a sigh from behind me. I thought it was you, but when I turned, no one was there." I sat shaking my head.

"Now that you've mentioned it, as I reached for my robe in the bathroom, I thought I heard someone take a breath and I looked to see if you had come into the room." She looked askance.

"Could it be Gregory doing this, trying a few spells to keep us off balance, or worried," I considered.

"I don't think so. He would just break in to get to me. He wants us complacent and unaware," she answered intelligently, and took a sip of the pop.

"I don't think he is capable of doing a 'spell of invisibility'. It would require much more energy than he could hold. We will have to keep our eyes open, though."

"Yes," I agreed.

"Frankie," Jojo said somewhat shyly.

"Yes, dear," I answered.

"Not to change the subject, but you don't have to keep sleeping on the couch." That said in a low, sultry voice.

"Oh! Where would you like me to be sleeping," I asked quite innocently.

"My bed?" She asked meekly.

"Will we actually get a chance to sleep in that bed?" I had risen and walked around the table to her.

"Well," a sheepish smile as she rose and fell into my arms, "maybe … after."

We kissed passionately, and then she led me to her bed, *our bed*. The house was secure; I switched off lights along the way and most of our clothing detailed the path to her bedroom; as to not be a hindrance to our lovemaking.

Laying face to face, *'closerthanthis'*; my arm cradled her neck; my head bent to kiss those beautiful lips as my other hand slid along her leg, looking to do devilish things between her thighs. My teeth nipped her bottom lip. I heard her breath quicken as my hand found its destination and did the happy dance.

Her one hand walked its way down to find her toy, quickening my breath as well. Her other hand reached between us, caressed my chest; elicited another response as sparks jumped from the act of her play with my nipples.

We kissed again.

Since enjoying it the last time, I nudged her atop me; her legs straddled my hips. There would be no games this time; I would take no prisoners. I bent my knees, entrapping her.

I felt the grasp, pull, and pulsations.

I tightened muscles, bringing a delicious sound from her throat. She controlled the rhythm, but I controlled the depth, at times, just barely and others to the very depths of our souls.

I watched her face, how her nostrils flared; and her hair swished back and forward with each heave of her body. Her chest and neck area flushed red, her eyes, dilated with the feelings that shivered through her being. Her neck muscles stiffened and relaxed as small orgasms erupted and subsided.

I saw how close she was, but not quite, not yet. She leaned forward, her hands on my chest.

I reached up, kissed her, whispered; 'sit up, lock your fingers together behind your head'.

She questioned me with a look. 'Do it, and enjoy'.

She sat back which caused her hips to widen, giving her the first surprise as I slid, yet deeper. The next surprise was the feeling she got as I ran my hands up her exposed sides and over her rock hard nipples. Her whole body tensed, her breath, ragged and quick, she fell forward in the throes of eruption, her pelvis bucked. I rose my hips, pushing deeper, trying to climb entirely inside.

She bit my nipple, I smacked her ass, and we both released together. We screamed, moaned, cried, and collapsed upon the bed buried in each other's arms, drained, and exhausted.

We lie there, contented.

For long minutes, nothing, but heaving chests as we each tried to get our breaths. She rolled off onto her side; I faced her, smiling. That same contented smile looked back at me.

We kissed lightly, once, twice.

"I love you," She whispered.

"I love you," I replied, happily.

My arm draped across her hip, facing, nose to nose, smile to smile, we slept, remembering nothing, until...

CHAPTER 24

A TAP!

A tapping upon my door. It was just an irritant, just above the quiet level; a disturbing tap, tap; tap, tap! At first, I thought the sink was dripping, but that was in the other direction.

I ruled out cat and dog since she had no pets. I was trying to be logical before waking her to some inane normal noise. I glanced at the time, *five am*.

I rose soundlessly.

My nine iron stood by the nightstand. Jojo didn't know where else to put it, so she leaned it against the wall.

I had nothing else large enough to use as a weapon that I could wrap my hands around, anymore. The golf club would have to do, I thought, as I got hold of it.

I tiptoed around the bed, reached slowly, mindful of where my foot was; not wanting to break a toe. Easily the knob turned in my hand; and with the club held high, I tore the door open.

It crashed loudly against the wall as I had begun my swing, to strike down on... no one!

Empty space stared back at me. The club bounced loudly off the carpet, the racket echoed through the hall.

Jojo screamed; *"WHAT THE HELL ARE YOU DOING?"*

I jumped at that noise, my heart pounded more.

Light flooded the room when she lit the lamp.

"Shush, shush, quiet." I tried to reassure, calm her.

"I heard a tapping on the door that went on for several minutes; thinking someone had broken in and I needed to stop them. But, there was nothing there."

She looked up with wild eyes and shook her head. "You were dreaming of ravens, crows; um... no, wood peckers," she insisted, and rose, "emphasis on the last word."

She patted my cheek and padded to the bathroom.

I shut the bedroom door, replaced the club against the wall in the event of further use.

I heard the water run, then the light click as she padded back to bed and got comfortable once again. I lay snuggled front to her back, once again relaxed.

"There was a tapping, you know," I stated, '*matter of fact*', as my arm once again draped across her bare hip.

"Sure," she answered sarcastically.

"There was," I whined, playfully.

"Go to sleep or no dessert tomorrow," she threatened giggling.

"Aw, shucks, there was," I chuckled.

She reached back and playfully smacked my ass with a laughing, "No!"

"Ouch," I yelled, mockingly, having fun with it.

A moment later, "OW," she yelled, differently. "No fair pinching the behind."

"I didn't pinch you," I informed her.

"Yes you did, right on the butt. I'm sure you left a mark," she complained.

"Let me see," I asked.

"No, not until we're married at least," she chided.

"No," I said sharply, touching her shoulder.

"Jojo, I didn't pinch you. Let me see."

She reached over to flip the lamp back on, moved to give me an unobstructed view, and pointed to the spot that hurt.

There was a bruise. I didn't know if it was a bedbug, mosquito or what.

I moved her hand away to get a better view.

"You have a welt, or bug bite," I informed her, reaching for my phone.

"Who are you calling," she demanded.

"No one, I want a photo," I said.

"Not on your life, Buster," she whined, covering the spot.

I moved her hand aside as I shot the picture.

"It is so you can more easily see. Get up."

"Why," she demanded.

"To check for bed bugs, mosquitoes, spiders; whatever bit you may still be here."

She moved her pretty ass fast after that.

"It felt like a pinch, not a bug bite," she insisted, looking at the photo.

We checked the entire bed, floor area, and room. Nothing we found could have caused that mark. We sat, naked, facing each other on the bed and wondered how the bruise appeared. There were no real answers, just speculation.

"It couldn't be Gregory, could it," I asked, exasperated.

"I don't see how. It would have to happen magickally, and we are protected from harmful, magickal spells," she reminded me. "We have the best protector in history; *MERLIN*."

"Some protector; Lancelot running off with Arthur's wife right under *MERLINS'* nose, and wasn't Arthur killed in battle," I joked. "Just kidding *MERLIN*; I know it was supposed to happen that way. I'm all for heading back to sleep," I suggested, yawning.

She stretched. "Yeah, another few hours would do me some good, too.

CHAPTER 25

We woke two hours later, unsure of what had plagued us. We smiled happily, showered in our own bathrooms, dressed, and met in the kitchen.

"Events are quickly coming to a conclusion," she said as we made breakfast.

Toast and coffee for me, she had tea and a corn muffin.

"How do you mean," I needed to know.

"It feels strange, almost as if… remember as a child, the summer coming to a close, that terrible thought of school starting; the end of vacation and you don't want the seasons to change? That's the feeling I get; an ending of some sort." With a quiet sigh, "It's scaring me."

"Maybe it is Gregory you feel," I offered, putting my arm around her as protection. "He is going to get desperate and make a straight on attack. He wants us to let our guard down, so he will wait as long as he can."

"And you will have your golf club ready 'FORE' him," she quipped. "I have a sense of humor too."

We sat opposite each other at the kitchen table, finishing our beverages. The chair to my left moved suddenly, sliding back. As if being pulled out for someone to sit. I did a double take, and then looked to Jojo. She stared at it, mouth agape.

I checked under the table to be sure we hadn't kick it by accident.

"Gregory, trying to move items, maybe trying to distract us; scare us; I don't know," as I rattled off suggestions. "Maybe poltergeist," I shrugged, I wasn't sure.

She stared with panic in her eyes, "Could that entity have left your house and come west," she whispered. "Could it be here doing these things, getting a feel for the house?"

"I don't know," I pondered.

"You don't know," she repeated back to me.

"YOU DON'T KNOW?" Panic rose a bit in her voice. "What do you know? Do you know any way to stop it?"

"You're the expert in all things paranormal," I gently reminded her. "Isn't there a cleansing we can do to rid the house of unwanted visitors? With all the tension, emotions, and power running rampant around here, isn't it more possible that we attracted a poltergeist? Maybe you could do a sage cleansing?"

"No, I wouldn't trust myself, I may miss something. One needs to be in the proper frame of mind, and I am not that serene!"

"There is an old friend, a psychic whom I think can help." After a few minutes, she was off the phone, an appointment made for later in the day.

"Seems my friend is getting rather old for this type of trouble. She will send her son."

"Maybe he can tell something about what is here, maybe get an impression," I suggested.

"We will see what he will find," Jojo stated. "Speaking of finding, come into the living room and see what I have," she prodded.

I rose and followed.

"Paul ordered these for my birthday a few years ago," pointing to a rack of CD's, "the hits of the 60's and 70's. *Carole King, Jim Croce, James Taylor, Temptations*; they are all here."

With the press of a button, strains of *John Lennon's 'Imagine'* came through the speakers. It took me back, us back, to a simpler time in life, in music and the genius of the lyrics. We stood, holding each other as the music played. *Pink Floyd* and *Elton* rocked. *The Moody Blues* did anything but make us that, while *Dawn*, featuring *Tony Orlando* told us *'To Tie a Yellow Ribbon.'* '*Ain't no Woman,*' sung the *Four Tops*, while another woman, *Gladys Knights* and her *Pips* rode a 'Train to Georgia' at midnight.

Standing there swaying, and sometimes singing along, everything was fine and dandy, like a *Hard-Candy Christmas!*

Then it happened; she came on! I lost it; I broke down in tears.

Jojo panicked, grabbing my hand, "Frankie, what's wrong. I thought you would love this."

"This song was the song that ripped me apart more quickly than any other. '*So Far Away'* by *Carole King* brought back memories, bittersweet. And '*Have you Seen Her,*' by *The Chi-lites*; were the two songs that ever reminded me of you. The memories, the sorrow, and the hopelessness came flooding back."

"In my mind, we could never be together, not without catastrophe, suffering, pain, sorrow, and death. After we would suffer all that, we could be together, if we could survive the guilt."

I sat on the floor, Jojo next to me, and I cried - for me - for her - for Judy and Paul.

"Frankie, we have gone through, are still going through it. It will work, we will survive because we are survivors, and there is no guilt for us to shoulder."

We sat for the final strains of the strings of James Taylor and the last notes of the piano by Carole. And all was quiet.

She broke the serenity of the moment,

"I think it is time to come back to the present and the real world," her hand lovingly caressed my arm.

I shook my head to clear my mind,

"Sometimes the past is so real and thick to me I can taste it, but it won't fill the stomach. We have several hours until your friend arrives, let's shop," I suggested.

I rose on shaky legs, helped her to rise and kissed the tears from her eyes and the words from her lips.

"Thank you my love!"

"What for," she shyly smiled back.

"For letting me wallow in the pains and miseries of the past for a bit. And then dragging me back when I was about to go over the precipice."

"Only because I love you, and I think I always have." She squeezed my hand.

We locked up the house and headed for the store.

"You know the diner will likely close now that we are shopping," Jojo mentioned as we pulled into the grocery parking lot.

"Maybe our booth will be donated to the Smithsonian for posterity," I quipped.

"Janet will be upset because of the tips she'll lose and may have to go on home relief," she laughed as we pushed the cart in through the automatic doors.

Some two hours and a few hundred dollars later we headed for home. The fun was just beginning; trying to see where most of those groceries would go.

It was her kitchen; I respected that and let her put purchases away, even if it made no sense for them to go where she stored them. She would have to live with it.

With that job out of the way, an easy lunch of canned soup made the day good. I loved 'Cream of Mushroom' with a side order of toast. For me, that was comfort food. I poured a cup of freshly brewed coffee and we sat to enjoy our meal.

The discussions ran to where we might live after all calmed and became quiet. I suggested we sell the homes, bank the money, and travel the country in a motor home. I could write anywhere; as long as we could connect to 'Wi-Fi', I had no troubles.

"You could be my co-writer again," was one idea.

She smiled, "my idea is when we find an area we like; we purchase a small home, or even a mobile home and keep it for part-time use. We could buy several around the country and travel."

"That is a marvelous idea," I replied.

She smiled and rose to close the icebox door. "I was sure I closed it tight when I put the groceries away," she cited.

"Perhaps something slipped and fell, pushing the door ajar," I questioned.

"I didn't see anything. Maybe I just thought I closed it."

We continued to straighten up, wash dishes, wipe tables, and do general cleaning.

"Who is the person coming and what beverage does he enjoy," I asked as I poured coffee.

"His Indian Name is 'Little Feather of The Wise Owl', but outside the tribe, they call him George. He's a tea drinker, but brings his own blend."

"Something like your brother did with the tobacco for the parties he and my sister used to attend," she chuckled.

"When I spoke to George's Mother, she was proud of his advancement of knowledge and tribal lore. That's why she asked him to come instead of her."

"His Mother is an Elder in the tribe," I asked.

"That would be a close analogy," she came to sit back at the table, grabbing a Mountain Dew on the way. A piercing shriek filled the room.

"*WHAT'S THAT NOISE,*" Jojo jumped.

"The kettle; I thought to heat water for tea," I stated, rising to shut the stove off.

CHAPTER 26

We enjoyed the quiet time. Though an occasional knock, rap, or slide of furniture intruded on our solitude. A louder knock caused us to jump from our skins.

"HELLO!" A deep voice rattled a few dishes.

"George, c'mon in, it's open," she called. We rose to meet him at the doorway.

George was a large man, more muscular than fat. He had long brown hair peppered with white strands tied in a ponytail. A big smile showed he enjoyed life and all that went with it. Jojo introduced me.

As I reached out in greeting, his eyes widened. Some Indians do not shake; it's a tribal taboo.

His arm rose as he said "How..."

I thought that maybe he was playing a joke, so I raised my hand, replying, "How!"

"No, look," he said, pointing his finger over my shoulder, into the kitchen.

I turned, as Jojo turned, to discover …

… Every cabinet door and drawer stood open, as was the icebox and the oven door. The dishwasher and the microwave doors also stood at attention.

I choked, she gurgled. We looked to each other with mouths opened.

I was the first able to speak, "c-ccome in George, if you dare."

"Yeah," finally finding her voice. "I think we have a slight problem that needs fixing."

She had begun closing doors, sliding drawers on one side of the kitchen; I did the other side, while George put the kettle back on to boil.

Quiet and still he sat to feel the house, the energies, and the powers.

I poured water for tea.

After a few minutes, he sighed, deeply.

I nearly choked on my coffee.

It didn't sound good, and the report he gave was not at all encouraging.

We sat talking, sipping beverages.

He explained that he would start the cleansing at the door with burning sage.

It did not sound safe; someone could be singed.

"Imagine it as a giant cigar made from 'Salvia Apiana,' or white sage. I call them 'smudges'." He explained.

With a wink, "I roll my own, and I hope I brought enough for the whole house."

He seemed distracted as he stood to prepare.

"What I will do is start outside the kitchen door with a self-cleansing. It will remove the negative and bad spirits from me. I use the feathers of the Owl, which is my 'spirit guide', to move the smoke into all areas. I use my voice and mind to alert the bad spirits that they are not wanted, not welcomed here."

"Joanna, will you smudge me to chase the bad spirits."

He stood, arms out, a large owl feather in each hand. He hummed something under the level of understanding. He was dancing; not realizing I think, of what he was doing.

I explained later what I saw. He said it was a tribal war dance.

Jojo moved the smoking leaves around him, from top to bottom, always in circular motions.

After several minutes, he opened his eyes.

"Thank you, Sister; your assistance was an asset. Please, place those leaves in the black pot on the floor in your kitchen. Their smoke will help provide additional cleansing."

His demeanor changed; his persona was, as if he were every Medicine Man from every Indian tribe. His face tightened to crinkled leather; his steps were as an Indian brave on the ridge, sure, slow, and rhythmic.

"I will work my way around each opening in every room; cleansing the space; cleansing the entrance; keeping unwanted spirits from taking residence," he instructed.

Starting at the kitchen door, the smudge stick gave off a not so unpleasant smell. Moving it in circular motions, he used his owl feathers to spread the smoke over a wider range, covering all places.

As he cleansed, he chanted, *"ANY AND ALL SPIRITS, ENERGIES, AND ENTITIES; LISTEN AND HEED! IF YOU ARE NOT OF THE LIGHT, YOU ARE NOT WELCOME HERE. BE GONE, BE GONE! IF YOU ARE NOT OF THE LIGHT, BE GONE, BE GONE! MOTE IT BE!"*

He demanded, cajoled, and threatened the bad spirits to leave. He continued around the kitchen and went into the hall.

Wherever a wall opened in a hall or doorway, he took it, eventually working his way through the entire house. All the rooms filled with the smell of burning sage; all the hallways and stairs clouded with the scented smoke.

"Isn't this what Joseph advised the other night?" I mentioned quietly. "I think we may even have some sage here in the house."

"Why are you whispering," Jojo questioned in a semi-low voice.

"Guess it is just a force of habit, a religious rite is going on, I whisper to show respect," I answered.

"Okay, I thought maybe you caught a cold," she replied.

"Why? Do I look sick? Is my color bad, are my eyes yellow," I asked, mocking dying coughs, chuckling.

"Shush," elbowing me softly in the ribs, "remember, Respect."

After nearly an hour, George was back.

As he put the 'Feathers' away, I asked, "Did you get a feeling of the spirit or entity?"

"It is not a friendly ghost, if that is what you want to know and also not very strong yet. It is newly come here, but will become familiar with the surroundings and grow in strength," he cautioned us. "I may have been in time."

"Could it be the spirit my Judy brought through," I queried.

The entire kitchen pulsated, the lights dimmed and brightened.

"What the hell was that," I gasped.

"Damned if I know," he responded.

"I don't know either,' Jojo said, "Is it possibly the ghost or poltergeist leaving?"

"NO! The sage cleansing would make it leave with a whimper; not that pulse," he mused.

Again, I asked, "But back to my original question, George."

"It might be. I would have to have more contact with it to know," he answered hesitantly, "but I do not think it wise to have that much contact with this spirit, if it still be here.

Having covered the entire home, he looked haggard and sat sipping tea. Jojo joined him, wanting to taste his special blend. I stuck with coffee.

Our conversation touched on the entity from my house. She thought it might have invaded here. I still wasn't sure and there was no way to tell without closer interaction, as George had stated.

He again offered his condolences to her, saying how sorry he was, and how he would miss Paul.

We shook hands as he readied to leave. She saw him out. The house was quiet and still.

Dinner would be a simple meal; and in addition, the first one we prepared as a 'couple'. A tossed salad with Italian Dressing, string beans with a touch of olive oil and butter, baked potato and steaks in the broiler.

I have had much practice cooking meals for different occasions and varying amounts of people, so I did my part and mainly stayed out of her way, just keeping an eye on the steaks.

Our first experience went perfectly. I kissed the cook. It was a pleasant meal, a quiet dinner.

We cleaned up and went to watch TV, trying to be a normal, everyday couple as we sat on the couch. The TV was on and there was an eye out for a demon and another eye out for a murdering warlock. Just the average, run of the mill couple.

I must have dozed.

I remembered opening my eyes and Jojo's head was on my lap facing the screen. I thought I heard a snore.

When I opened my eyes again, it was to a different show, she was face up, eyes closed, and I did hear a snore, but it probably was from me.

I shook her shoulder, "C'mon babe, let's head for bed. We need our sleep."

She shrugged my hand off, told me to leave her alone, or to go take a flying something or other. Not a particularly pleasant person to waken.

Again I shook her shoulder; an eye opened; a half smile crossed her lips, "Is it morning, already?"

Bending, I kissed those lips. "No dear, it is bedtime; come along."

I shut the TV, helped her to stand and guided her to the room. She began to undress as I headed for my bathroom. In just a few minutes, both tucked in, goodnight kisses given, and we were going to sleep, this time.

CHAPTER 27

I awoke to a glorious day. We jumped out of bed, wished each other a good morning. I had showered, shaved and dressed in record time and was just leaving my bathroom when I heard a loud scream, followed by an expletive echo through the house.

I have not moved that fast in years.

Jojo stood in the entrance of the kitchen; her hand at her throat, I think with a death grip on MERLIN. I looked passed her to see every door and drawer open, and in addition, the chairs piled on the kitchen table and counters.

Calming slightly, she was next on the phone to George, wanting to know what he was going to do about it.

"I'll refund your money," he joked through the speakerphone.

"You never gave me a bill," she squawked.

"That's what I mean. I am trying to get you to calm down and think. It is stressful right now, for good reason, yes. Be unstressed Sister Joanna. Breathe in and out, okay, good."

"Now, let me call another friend to see what he can do. I will have him there as soon as possible. Be calm," he advised.

"Sure, easy for you to say; you aren't looking at all the doors and drawers open all over the kitchen and the chairs piled up on the ..." she was having a meltdown.

"Okay George, thanks for the help", I interjected. "She will be fine. I'll call and tell you how we make out."

"You're welcome, you will take good care of her, I know. There is nothing to worry as long as you two are together. *'Blessed Be'*, my friends." He hung up.

My arms encircled her, to reassure, to calm. Things were not easy, yet. I pulled a chair down onto the floor, and let her sit.

I tried to shut the doors, but could not get free from her grip.

She looked up at me with that beautiful face; I bent to wipe a tear away with my finger' and we were in each other's arms again.

We just stood there holding each other.

I hadn't imagined a hug could feel so great, so fulfilling. The energy flowed both ways; giving us indescribable feelings of contentment and safety. I have not felt a hug like that since we first reconnected on her front lawn those short years ago.

We eventually let go with the satisfaction of knowing that we could do that all we wanted, later. It was better than sex … nearly!

Putting the kitchen back to right, I was most certain now, this was the entity from my house.

We had a quick breakfast, jumping at every little noise, then got the dishes cleaned. We sat to take a breath when a loud buzz startled me. I nearly had a stroke, while she went to answer the front doorbell. I followed up the rear, so to speak.

"Hello, Mrs. James. I am Father Braden and this is Johnny, my altar boy. May we come in? George sent us, said it was urgent."

"Pleased to meet you," she stepped back to let them pass. "This is Frank Johnson."

"Hello," I greeted, "are you sure it is all right to bring the boy. George did tell you what was going on in here?"

"I have known George for a goodly number of years; agreeable chap, but tends to exaggerate a bit," the Good Father explained. "But it is nice to meet you," nodding to me. "George mentioned something about you over the phone," he admitted.

"Yeah," Johnny stated, "he said you were a witch."

The Priest gave the lad a look. "I must apologize for the boy."

And after a sigh, "Johnny, not everything you hear is true, and most of it should not be repeated."

"Sorry Father, sorry Mr. Johnson," he apologized sincerely.

"That's quite all right, Johnny," I said as I put my hand on his shoulder. "Can we get you something, tea, milk, cookies," I offered.

And agreeable nod from the Priest.

I retrieved refreshments while she filled The Good Father in on what had transpired. He sat with his back to the kitchen and enjoyed coffee and a cookie.

Johnny opted for Mountain Dew; I slipped a few extra cookies onto a plate for him. He was fourteen and would play football again this year.

The Priest asked about our upbringings, and why we thought the house was haunted. We answered courteously, again explaining what had happened.

"I am of the belief that all hauntings have logical explanations," he postured with a sip of his coffee and a nibble of the cookie.

At last, "Johnny, be a good lad and bring in the satchel. Thank you."

And then to us, "Most homes of suspected possession are something like shaking pipes, overactive imaginations, or drug and alcohol abuse."

He was not paying attention to where we stared, but just caught up in his own little diatribe. So, it surprised him when Johnny came back in, dropped the bag in the doorway and cried, *"OH SHIT!"* in a loud and frantic voice, followed by another expletive.

"*JOHNNY*," the Priest began stormily as he turned towards the boy. Something peculiar in his peripheral vision caused him to complete the turn to face the kitchen. His mouth fell open, his eyes went wide and he squeaked out an "*OH, SHIT*," or two of his own, as every door and drawer was again opened.

He halfway rose, reaching up for his Crucifix on his chest as his chair toppled backwards and slid slowly across the floor to jump up atop the counter.

I walked over to lend moral support to the boy, but the kid had more moxie than I thought. He had picked up the bag and squeaked, "We should begin, Father," as he removed the items needed for the Blessings.

Father Braden nodded, picked up his Scapular, kissed it, and with shaking hands, placed it around his neck. He retrieved the Holy Water and Sprinkler, "let's begin". A deep breath helped to steady him.

He started by blessing himself, then Johnny and lastly, Jojo and I. Prayers were next and then he moved on to the actual Blessing. It was similar to the sage cleansing, excepting for the use of Holy Water in place of the smoke.

They moved through the house, praying, and sprinkling the Water. Surprisingly, he made it through the entire home without running. He gave the pentagram and the altar a wide berth.

Johnny was extremely brave. When the growling started and I told him we did not have any pets, I thought he was going to faint, or run.

We prayed prayers I hadn't uttered aloud in years.

We thanked him for all his work, and I praised Johnny especially, as he packed up the implements of The Blessing.

Jojo saw them to the door.

The house seemed quiet and peaceful, but there was still a warlock against whom to defend. We collected up all the crystals and spent the day arranging them on the altar. She put some power into them to speed the charging, though I didn't want her rejuvenating them all. I was afraid it would deplete her energies dangerously low.

I searched further on the internet, tracking down websites, looking for spells and protections that might keep an evil warlock at bay.

We finished at sunset. It had been a long, trying day and she looked as if she would fall over.

"Why don't we go out for dinner instead of all the bother of cooking," I suggested.

She thought it a marvelous idea.

Janet was back from her days off, filled with life and energy. We three had a good evening and an enjoyable time. Afterward, we wandered through Shoppe's and stores, picked up a few incidentals and, overall, did a great job to find ways to delay our return home.

My fear was the Priest did not rid us of that which visited; mimicking Jojo's thoughts.

Hesitantly, I unlocked the door; she recycled the alarm and found everything quiet and serene. We checked through the basement and garage; I even checked the kitchen, twice. Nothing was amiss. Maybe The Blessing did rid us of our houseguest.

We spent a relaxing time watching TV and another quiet night snuggled together, in bed. Well, I was nearing 60 years old.

'There maybe snow on the rooftop, but there is fire in the furnace,' is true. Just, that once in a while the fire damped down to just a smolder. Tonight, sadly was another of those more frequent nights.

CHAPTER 28

Awakening the next morning, we were rested, happy, and ready for anything.

I had not made pancakes in a long while, so I mixed the batter and Jojo prepared coffee and side dishes of fresh fruits. She had never tried my flapjacks and was highly impressed.

"What all is in here," she queried, pointing to the second stack of steaming, moist cakes with her fork.

"Just a few household ingredients in their proper proportions," I told her.

She seemed surprised, to say the least; and I was to be full of surprises even I didn't know about, yet.

We heard the first loud thump while working with the crystals on the altar in the basement. We went to investigate, apprehensive of what we might find. With the doors locked, and the alarm set, no one could just wander in.

We looked through the house and discovered the noise emanated from the bedroom. The closet door slammed as we entered. Several items on her dresser quivered; not good when one was a scissor.

Jojo thought she might communicate with it, placate it, and maybe even get it to leave. I wasn't so sure, and didn't want her risking her health and well-being.

I found that I had no say in the matter.

We wended our way to the kitchen, a sense that that was the focal point of the haunting.

She sat relaxed, deep breaths to clear her mind. Another deep breath and;

'THE SPIRIT IN THE HOUSE, WE MUST COMMUNICATE!'

A door slammed somewhere.

"YOU ARE NOT WANTED HERE," she ordered loudly, another thump as if something thrown.

"YOU MUST LEAVE," she commanded.

Her chair slid violently sideways. Good thing I was nearby to grab her before she and the chair slammed into the wall.

The CD player started, Carole sang 'So far away'. Then the speed changed, as if playing a 45 RPM record at a 78 RPM speed. Then changed again, faster, until it was nothing but a high-pitched squeal, faster even than a 'Chipmunk Song'. It stopped, a deathly silence echoed through the house. The disc ejected, the speakers hissed loudly, ***"GET OUT NOW."***

Jojo sat there, stoic, *"NO,"* she answered resolutely.

"THIS IS MY HOME!"

As an aside, she asked me to call Joseph and explain our problem.

"LEAVE NOW," she again warned, *"OR WE WILL BRING IN ONE THAT WILL CHASE YOU BACK WHENCE YOU CAME."*

A door slammed upstairs and we heard something else rattle, besides my knees. I closed the phone and informed her that Kyra would be here this afternoon. We should find something to do elsewhere, but more importantly, Jojo was to tell the entity what Kyra had repeated to me.

I had written out the short script and handed it over. She glanced down, and to the entity:

"WE ARE LEAVING; BUT NOT BECAUSE YOU COMMAND; BUT TO BRING BACK SOMEONE WHO WILL SEND YOU TO YOUR DAY OF RECKONING!"

A shudder, almost of fear ran through the house, tumbling me off my feet.

"What was that," I asked rhetorically, using the table to pull myself upright.

Jojo shrugged.

I checked that all was secure, set the alarm and locked the door.

There was time to kill; the suggestion was a visit to the local movie house.

I agreed, "Great idea, I haven't been to the movies since I was a kid," I exaggerated.

She took my hand, looked me in the eye and in a very serious voice, "You had better prepare dear, 'They have 'talkies' now."

We both laughed as I pulled out of the driveway, anticipating the enjoyment of a few hours in the theater.

They were running an afternoon matinee special of John Agar films. We had our choice of "She Wore a Yellow Ribbon," "Fort Apache," or "Tarantula."

It was a hard decision to pick the movie we probably weren't going to watch, anyway.

"Tarantula" won. I remembered that she didn't like scary movies, and abhorred spiders. Thinking the more times she was frightened, the more times she would be holding on to me.

I saw more action in the balcony that afternoon then Agar and John Wayne saw in 'She Wore a Yellow Ribbon."

Just after three pm we headed back. I was thinking this was going to be a bumpy ride.

My phone rang.

Jojo answered it.

After a brief conversation, she replaced it in my shirt pocket.

"Kyra is on the way."

"How does she know where we live," I asked.

"She knows," was the answer.

CHAPTER 29

I parked on the driveway.

The house felt hushed, anxious, its energies held for one last attempt at ...

We didn't wait long; a car pulled up next to mine.

As we entered, the quiet expectation continued. Kyra asked for a glass of water and headed to the basement. She didn't ask where it was, but walked softly, opened the basement door and descended to the altar and pentagram.

With a quick look, and a compliment on the arrangement, she inscribed a few new sigils on the floor with chalk from her pocket. Then collapsed easily into a relaxed lotus pose in the center of the pentagram. The water glass went between her legs on the floor.

She began to hum, concentrating on the glass.

A voice came from her, but not sounding like her. The words were indistinguishable. We heard a sound like a quiet bell, barely discernible. However, Kyra heard and answered again; for half an hour this continued, nothing that we could interpret, nothing distinguishable or intelligible.

She tensed, she cried; muscles in spasm as if in a fight for her life. Her eyes opened in wild fright to close slowly in serene composure.

Suddenly stiffening; she fell sideways in a faint, then pushed herself slowly upright.

With a tired smile, she revealed a strange crystal tightly clasped in her hand.

Not the usual color stone we use for power, but jet-black; so dark it hurt the eyes. She placed it in the middle of the consecrated area.

To look upon it was troubling.

"I have entrapped the entity in this place; it is harmless for the moment."

We helped her up the stairs and into the kitchen where she sat quiet, calm, her strength rejuvenating. A few sips of tea to help regain sensibilities.

Finally, sitting up straighter, and with a deep, calming breath; "It would be impossible to relate what all transpired. Some of our conversation was on a different level entirely."

As the explanation continued and the events retold, we soon realized Kyra was a strong psychic and a very old soul.

"This is the entity that was in your house, Frank. Your spirit calmed, steadied, and became a beacon. It felt that and tracked you here. Its sole purpose is killing when called. When no victim surfaces, it turns on the one who summoned it."

Looking at the expression on my face, frowning, "I am sorry, but at times, when in the workings of demons, reality is harsh."

She stopped for another sip of tea.

"The entity was created in an area near Canton, China about 500 AD. This soul, accused of crimes she did not commit, remanded to the executioner for beheading."

"A stranger materialized in the little girl's cell. The child, already frightened beyond reason, fell to her knees thinking the stranger a god."

"He named himself, 'The Magician', making a pact; a promise of life and salvation in exchange for her power, a covenant upon which she swiftly agreed."

"The youngster did not know the power transferred at time of death. As her head hit the ground, The Magician, psychically full, cursed the spirit of the little girl to an eternity of suffering and pain."

"Now, forced to roam the earth, this entity captures souls and powers of the newly deceased. She holds those spirits, the ones she had to take and the ones The Magician killed, and used those energies to foster her hatred, to search out the spirit that is 'The Magician'."

A smile at Jojo while Kyra took another sip of tea.

I jumped in, "You keep saying, 'she'; this entity is Female and a child?"

"At the time of death, 'Lian', as she was named was less than 10 years old," Kyra answered. "And spirits can be masculine or feminine. The bodies here in this life can be either, but the spirit never changes. You may have a Masculine body here, but your spirit could be feminine."

The look on Jojo's face begged another whole story. "The spirit that this entity is looking for, 'The Magician' is here in the body of Gregory," she probed, shaking her head in disbelief.

"Yes," Kyra confirmed. "Once the entity began moving this way, it sensed the old energy of 'The Magician' along the secret routes."

It confused me. "If the magician had the power from the little girl, why would he bother to curse her and not just let her go in peace?"

Kyra explained, "The last traces of energy would be that of 'The Magician', so the death would be recorded as from him. Once you step over the boundary of too many deaths in your name, you are called to pay for what you have wrought. He uses the entity to store the spirits, making him unaccountable," she finished.

"Then he can kill at will and no punishment befalls him," I queried.

"And the entity now wants Gregory," Jojo asked her question on top of mine.

"Yes," Kyra agreed, "to both. Remember, this entity gathers spirits along the way; not solely the ones she is responsible for, but also the ones he takes. And between the two, the numbers are staggering.

"Wait!"

Kyra looked at my frown and nodded.

"If this entity holds the spirits it takes, then…"

She nodded again to me.

"So, Judy's spirit is here in this house?"

This time, a smile.

I stopped to get my head around what I just confirmed. That was why the house shuddered when I mentioned my wife's name. Then the other light went on. I looked to Jojo, who gave me a double take as tears formed in her eyes, as well.

"Can we contact Paul … and Judy," Jojo beseeched, "Are their spirits all right. Can we communicate with them?" She had many questions that begged answers.

"The spirit is that stone, trapped, it can do or show nothing. It can communicate with me, but nothing else. It has no fear, save its fear of me, so it will do no harm or damage for now. Its power is hidden and trapped as long as it stays within the pentagram," Kyra stated.

She looked to Jojo and nodded. "Now, you can be sure of what Paul felt. Truly, the warlock killed him. Paul's spirit here is proof."

"So their spirits are not at rest," Jojo stated hesitantly, not really wanting to hear. "They are destined to spend eternity with that ... that thing?" I could see her getting unnerved, intensely upset over that thought.

She finally turned to Kyra, "Is there anything we can do? Can't we, well, maybe," I saw the wheels begin to turn inside her head, "maybe make a deal with her. Bring Gregory to her, in exchange for her letting go those poor souls?"

Kyra looked at her, one brow rose; her eyes grew wide which begot a broad smile. We felt the energy in the room change, the closeness of the entity. Kyra stiffened, sat rigid, stared deep into ...

After several moments, just mere heartbeats,

"... It is done! You get Gregory with-in these walls and she will un-leash all the souls she has tethered to her," Kyra explained before neatly collapsing into a heap.

Jojo reached over to grab her.

"Help me get her down the hall; she can rest on the couch in my office for the time being."

We sat, formulating a plan to get the Warlock into the house; preparing for what we hoped, prophetically would not be the final battle for us. He must be kept here long enough to let the Entity out and get to his, um… the Magicians' spirit.

I walked down to the basement. The power crystals on the altar held a charge and needed to be upstairs.

I felt the pull of the Black Crystal. It called for freedom, begged for release. It sat in the middle of the Pentagram, pulsating with power.

I almost wanted to let it out, but knew Gregory would feel it and never come near the house. I felt its pain, its torment. The centuries it roamed freely, now trapped in the stone, in the Circle. I felt the other spirits, expectantly awaiting release as well. Hurriedly I climbed the stairs.

The entity was still sentient enough that it felt pain, suffering, and guilt; and made others cry for it.

Jojo was upset with the knowledge that Paul and Judy were prisoners, not able to move on, to turn the page, so to speak.

We sat on the couch trying to come to grips with the tasks before us, the enormous responsibility to free those souls. She snuggled up under my arm, her head rested on my chest. I reached my left hand up to brush the single tear from her cheek. Her hand grasped at mine, held it. A sob escaped from her pretty, little lips.

CHAPTER 30

Another sound then, a crackle, a grating voice boomed through the room,

"WHAT A TOUCHING SCENE."

My head snapped up, Jojo's a second later; a figure, clad in dark, heavy robes, jewelry hung from him everywhere making him immediately recognizable; 'Gregory', 'The Magician.'

"NOW BITCH, you have nowhere to run. That puny husband of yours was no match for me. He almost didn't know what was happening," the warlock shouted.

"This replacement you picked will be even easier," he sneered.

I guess he referred to me. I bounded to my feet, shielding her from him. The look he saw in my eyes was hopefully a confidence that I didn't feel. I needed to distract him long enough for her to get to the basement.

His hands came up, fingers curled to strike.

"FIRST YOU, OLD MAN. I will let her watch you grovel and beg before you die, then the bitch will be mine. She'll pay for running away."

His fists descended; the power surged, crackled about his fingers. I watched as the bolt formed on his hand; pure white lightning danced, causing the hairs on his arms to rise. I watched as the power sizzled across the room; the smell of ozone thick in the small space caused my eyes to water as the bolt smashed into my chest.

A bright flash as it contacted my body, blinding me for a moment. Surprisingly, nowhere the amount of agony that I thought I would feel dying.

Actually, none at all.

I looked down, expecting to see a gaping hole, to feel shooting pain as the magicks should have ripped my body apart. I took a short step back to maintain my balance, noticing the small burn mark on my shirt.

He glowered at me, bewildered, anticipating a different reaction. Expectations of me writhing and screaming, begging him to finish me.

I felt Jojo's hands at my back as she helped me stay upright. Surprise in her voice as well, as she saw the power course through me and be… absorbed.

"BLESSED BE, YOU'RE A WITCH," she exclaimed.

"Fine time to be calling me names," I replied without a second thought.

"So, you have some power; at least it makes my ultimate victory more of a challenge," he boasted.

"Try for the basement," I whispered with a backward glance.

A nod, a quick hug around my waist and she was off and attained the cellar door by the kitchen.

Gregory, seeing her, and where she headed, sensed the altar. Reaching out his hand in a grasping motion, she froze in place.

"You remembered my fear of the ATHAME. You know that Blessed Knife would send my spirit on a journey for an eternity of suffering and anguish."

"YOU WILL NOT MAKE IT," He screamed.

His hand went up, fist clenched. Jojo's body rose several inches from the carpet, flew backwards to slam hard into the wall.

I heard the whoosh of air leave her lungs and the thud as her skull hit. Her eyes rolled back into her head as she slid to the floor, barely conscious.

So much for *MERLIN* and his protections.

Gregory turned back to me, tossing spell after spell. With powerful walls of energy he tried to beat me into submission.

More powerful bolts sizzled across the room; sounds of deep vibrations assailed my ears. His entire arsenal of spells and tricks just to defeat me.

I held both my palms up, to repel the powers, surprised that I still stood.

Finally accepting that I was a Witch.

I sensed that the dark crystal Jojo wore powered me. *MERLIN* helped to protect me, protect her.

A movement by the door, another distraction. A quick look, Detective John and Sergeant Bob Adams crowded the opening; several police officers jockeyed for position behind them, guns drawn. They could get no further into the room.

John strained to reach Jojo; it was as if a physical wall held them back. I watched as he grasped his crystal; his shoulders hunched, pushing hard against that which no one else saw. It looked as if he uttered a pray or mouthed a spell. And at last, with a final try, he managed the two steps needed. Frantically, with a few fingers, he snared her sweater, yanking her to safety.

Sgt. Adams helped carry her back to the waiting EMT's.

My attention diverted, Gregory threw his most powerful curse. Frustration adding fuel to his spell, it knocked me backwards. I slammed into the couch and wall. The cushions partially protected me from serious harm, but the distraction was enough to give him the upper hand.

Slightly dazed, a bit confused, a movement from the other hallway diverted my attention yet again. My thoughts switched to Kyra resting in the office.

A jet-black cat with gold flecked-eyes ran from the hall, darting between us. The basement door opened before her.

Gregory laughed, *"Even the animals are deserting you,"* as he moved the few steps towards me. His hands rose to strike that killing pose.

Mine went up in self-defense; hoping that somehow I could use powers I never knew I had in ways I never knew I could.

After all, *I was a WITCH!*

A triumphant sneer curled his lip; in a moment, he knew he would have victory.

I needed time to think, to buy time for the cat to unleash the entity. Even though it might cost me my life, Jojo would be safe; Judy and Paul's spirits would be freed.

My mind, a thought conjured from nowhere; aloud I yelled, ***"MAGICIAN, PREPARE TO MEET THY DOOM."***

"What… But how?" The look on his face changed to one of deeper questioning; then wonder and finally to actual, sheer terror.

"NO, NOOO! IT CAN'T BE," he shrieked.

A mournful wail, like none ever heard in this realm screeched from the basement, rising in pitch and intensity, vibrating the very essence of our cores.

"NO, you are DEAD, cursed long ago. Keep away, KEEP AWAY," his voice, sheer terror.

A dark shadow moved on him, a mist descending from the ceiling, continued growing, expanding.

"You can't have found me, keep away, please?"

It moved closer, forcing him further into the corner of the room, giving him no place to hide, nowhere to run. He tried spells to divert it, to move it. He tried to stop it, reason with it. He begged on quaking knees; but it moved on him. He slithered farther back, turned, arms up in supplication. The mist never slowed, but settled down around him. Bit by bit he disappeared, consumed by that - Thing.

I crawled towards the kitchen, keeping low to avoid connection with the dark mass.

I saw down the cellar stairway, the cat about to bound upward; then Jojo behind me. I glanced back to be sure she was all right and received a relieved smile.

Kyra stood at the top of the stairs licking her lips. We stared as the grotesque scene unfolded in the living room, too gruesome to watch, too enthralling to turn away.

Gregory disintegrated; his skin and blood just flotsam, dissolved by the mist. The screams of panic, pain, and terror gurgled from his throat. His body writhed, heaved as the darkness took him.

The wail of the mist became another noise, another cry.

A cry of *triumph*!

It joined Gregory's final shrieks; piercing our skulls, blurring our visions, causing hands to cover ears. It grew louder, windows vibrated, walls and floors quaked, and the last that was Gregory disappeared within the mist, with one last pitiful scream.

And then complete and utter silence.

We all collapsed from the strain of pushing against that, which was no longer there.

With help, I stood groggily between John and Bob. I felt Jojo, her hand on my arm to steady me. Her eyes going over all the blood and contusions that adorned my body.

Questions arose among the police officers, "what just happened?"

"Is everyone all right?"

"What was that?"

"What the hell is going on?"

I heard at least one officer be sick.

Again, the wail rose, windows rattled, the walls pulsated as if taking a breath. I heard a police officer behind me; "Shit! This can't be good."

Another voice; I don't know if the utterance came from Kyra, or Jojo, "Just wait; it gets better."

Hands tried to pull us back. Sgt. Bob stood in abject terror.

The dark mist returned, sliding down the walls, descending from the ceiling; roiling, spinning, the light not totally blocked; but weighing upon us in heaviness of the spirit.

And then

A leaf swirled through the room.
A small leaf.

It slid in the air though no breeze bestirred it.
A pretty leaf.
A leaf the color of fall, and the room brightened, and our spirits lightened.

A second leaf joined the first, also pretty, and the room lightened more. Then a third danced on still air. And slowly, as we stood in wonder, leaves filled the room, as if autumn invaded with a myriad of colors, shapes and sizes to bedazzle us.

The sound of laughter, as the tinkling of a bell touched our senses. The dance continued, leaves moved one way, then another, always clockwise, but never the same motion. At times, a single leaf caught our attention, and then a swirl of hundreds, thousands beautifully choreographed drew us in. The sense of joy, of freedom, came as a lilt on the air.

The leaves, in singles, than twos and threes drifted through the walls, or up through the ceiling.

I caught the feel; spirits departing; free to turn the page. I looked to Jojo; the realization already had dawned in her eyes as tears streamed down her cheeks. The sense of relief as the souls tasted freedom, released, some after centuries of confinement.

I wiped my eyes, cleared my vision. A sagacity of relief and joy flooded through us all.

Then two leaves danced in front of us. Two!

I knew, Judy and Paul's last thoughts to us; *'Be well, remember us; good life; Blessed Be!'*

Jojo sobbed. She knew now as I did, there was no reason for guilt.

The two leaves drifted away, spinning together, intertwined. They moved through the wall, their adventure continuing.

And, finally, a last leaf.

The littlest, prettiest leaf danced daintily on air in front of Sergeant Bob.

We sensed the spirit of a little girl.

'Daddy! It's okay Daddy. You tried to save me. He was bad. Now he is punished.'

The voice was a tinkling, very quiet, barely a whisper.

Bob was motionless, mouth agape; tears streamed down his cheeks.

"ABBY?"

He wept, nearly silent, more of a hushed sigh. His hand reached, barely brushing that colorful spirit. A spark danced across to him; laughter of a little girl filled the room.

'It's okay Daddy, I love you!' The leaf trembled a last good-bye, slowly rose up through the roof, and twirled its way to her own unfolding.

Bob stood there, smiling though he wept.

The tinkling of earlier drowned out the quiet sobs. Kyra stiffened as the entity again brought the ugliness to the room. Her eyes, unfocused, tried to stare; darted left, then right; suddenly rolled up to the back of her head. A gurgle escaped her lips.

John and I grabbed her as she fell.

Other hands helped carry her back into the kitchen.

The entity dissipated.

CHAPTER 31

I noticed ringing sounds again.

The entity back? No. The alarm system ringing; I went to deactivate it.

Kyra lie on a gurney as an EMT checked to be sure she was well. Her eyes fluttered open as the good-looking medico stood over her.

Smiling up, she purred.

He returned the smile, forgot what he was doing, and helped her to her feet.

Detective John released the police and EMT's back to regular duty.

At the end, those few of us who remained sat around the kitchen table. More questions than answers flew about the room. I poured coffee and dished out cookies.

Jojo handled the tea and Mountain Dew.

Bob sat, coffee untouched, yet unable to talk.

Kyra took his hand. He looked up and the floodgates released again. His emotions piled up and then tore down. He sobbed helplessly for minutes. She stood there with him; let go his hand, proffered a napkin.

"Thank you. This was the first time I have cried since my baby disappeared those few months ago. I have not been able to think of that day, or even know what exactly happened until now.

He took a deep breath to steady himself, waved Jojo off.

"I have to tell this now," he whispered.

"Abby was our daughter. She was our world, and extra-special as a child. The baby we were not supposed to have."

"My wife, Annie, couldn't conceive. That was the doctor's prognosis. Then the miracle of Abby. She was our life."

"A man lured her away." A tear again glistened his cheek.

"She and Annie enjoyed time together in the park down the street from our home. She was five and would swing, while my wife would enjoy the fresh air and read."

"Annie called me, frantic; she had looked down to her book. When she turned back, the swing still moved, but was empty. Thinking she jumped as children are wont to do, she called out. Not hearing Abby, she yelled, then screamed for her."

"But she was gone!"

"My wife questioned parents, other children; no one knew anything, no one saw her."

"Finally, one shy, little girl pointed to the trees, told of a big man wearing a dark robe."

"We searched the rest of the day and night, with no luck. We placed messages on websites, the TV news ran stories, and where ever people congregated we put the word out."

His hand grasped the coffee mug hard; I thought it would implode from the force.

"We did a house to house search with no results. We finally got lucky when an anonymous tip mentioned a certain car. I followed the lead and found it parked in a driveway near a rundown bungalow."

He stopped, tears formed again. He sipped the coffee.

I wished I had something stronger to give him.

"I didn't wait for back-up, but quietly went in and found a makeshift altar and a Pentagram. At the time, I did not know the difference between upside down and right side up. All I saw was my little girl, dismembered, lying on the cold, dirty floor."

"The 'son-of-a-bitch' walked in, saw me and dissolved right in front of my eyes as I aimed my weapon. My partner had heard my yells and the shots, broke in the front door and watched as the man disappeared in front of us, unharmed."

Bob was near to breaking down again.

"That bastard left my poor little girl dead, manacled, and cut apart. Why?"

He looked around, as if in expectation of an answer. "Why? C-c-can someone tell me, please," almost whispered.

He looked up at Kyra; a lost, little boy look on his face; tears sprouted again. She reached over and touched his forehead.

His head drooped, chin against his chest. Eyes closed slowly, fluttered, anguish on his face, a quick, "WHY?" turned into a long sigh.

"He'll sleep a bit," she informed us, moving his coffee so it wouldn't spill. "When he wakes, some of the pain will be eased."

"What exactly happened to cause Gregory to take his daughter," Jojo asked, tears still misted in her eyes.

"She was a conduit as you, but with much more power," Kyra began. "He couldn't resist, was drawn to her like a magnet draws metal. He felt her a long way off; and he traveled far to reach her," she continued.

"I felt her power when she came through to her dad inside. Her great energy is how she got through to here."

"When Gregory kidnapped her, she nearly killed him. He had no choice but to slay her or die." She stopped for a moment to sip tea.

"Unlike you, she was able to use her powers and he couldn't control her." Another pause to take another breath, getting her emotions back under control.

"What's going to happen with him, now," Jojo asked.

"Bob will go home, hug Annie, and as he does, some of what he felt will be imparted to her. She will feel some of the healing and completion. They spoke to divorce lawyers; each blamed the other for what happened, and worse, they each blamed themselves. Now they can better decide how to face the future," she finished.

Jojo had hold of my hand, both of us still misty-eyed. Not for what we went through, but for Bob, Annie, little Abby and what they won't have because of what was 'The Magician'.

We now know we have no reason to feel guilt.

At a knock on the door, I jumped, startled. Surprisingly, Joseph stood there, or not so surprising.

I invited him in; someone had already retrieved a Mountain Dew. We sat and got comfortable.

"Now," I began. "There are a few thousand questions I need answered."

Jojo shook her head and groaned, Kyra and the rest just laughed.

"WHAT?" I queried.

"Go ahead and ask away," Joseph prompted.

"Kyra, what else did the entity say to you at the end? I know I felt gratitude from it; but, what else?"

She and Joseph looked at me, brows narrowed as if just seeing me for the first time.

"She was happy to release her captives. As a prisoner in the crystal, she learned how entrapment felt, she knew the pain and sorrow she caused the spirits and felt grief, and regret," Kyra admitted.

"I feel sorry for her," Jojo lamented. "Being trapped with The Magician for an eternity is not what should happen and being just a child, well, isn't there something that can be done to help alleviate her suffering?"

Kyra looked at me.

I nodded. "Even though the entity took Judy, it had no choice; the curse being what it was. It sounds cruel, but Judy is in a better place, and with others who also deserve their rewards."

I nodded again, smiling at Kyra, "If we can help Lian somehow, let's do it."

She sat and thought; "there is a way. We will hold a service the night of the next full moon. We might be able to separate them, move his curse from her to him and then make him powerless to interact with this world, or any other. He would see and hear, but could not affect change."

That sounded great; a fit punishment for someone that caused such pain and misery.

Bob came back to the world of the living, his emotions a little better under control. Letting out all that pent up sorrow is good for the healing process.

He looked sheepish. "Sleeping on duty is not good for the image of a police sergeant," he smiled wanly.

John made a show of checking his watch, "You've been off duty for the last hour, Bob. It's all good. Go home and talk with your wife."

He nodded, smiled when he looked at Kyra. "I don't know how to thank you," he said with all sincerity, tears brimmed his eyes. "And how do I explain to Annie about …"

Kyra silenced him with a finger on his lips. "Annie will feel what you felt; hear, and sense all that you did," she related. "Just go home, hug her tight, and let what happens, happen."

He said quiet good-byes and departed.

"That was why he wanted nothing to do with the case when we mentioned witches and such," Jojo exclaimed. "It hit too close to home."

We sat for several more minutes all trying to let this sink in.

A thought came to me. "Hey, wait a minute," I interrupted the quiet. "Gregory boasted that only the consecrated knife could harm and ultimately send him to Hell, or worse. Yet it still sits in the basement. What happened," I asked, as I looked right at Kyra.

"Well," Joseph began to explain, amused, "Gregory was a bit confused, I am not sorry to say. He mentioned the definition of what he thought could hurt him. In reality, it was '*ATHAME*'."

"That Holy Knife was so named, long ago, to honor an ancient spirit that helped in times of trouble." He cleared his throat a bit, as he finished.

Jojo put all the pieces together. Joseph and Kyra *ATHAME*, and since it was the cat who moved the stone out of the Circle, she unleashed the entity that caused the demise of the Magician.

John had gone to see about some officers out front.

I glanced to Kyra and smiled. "I'll never tell." I said, "I promise."

"Never tell what," she purred, double blinking those gold-specked eyes at me.

CHAPTER 32

It took several days for Jojo and me to recuperate from the effects of the attack. We spent time resting, sleeping, talking and just holding each other.

I awoke one morning; the sun streamed in through the window and it felt good. I rose quietly, to not awaken her. It had been several weeks since I had had the time to fully relax.

I wandered out to the back yard.

There was a hidden corner with a soothing quality about it, a quietness. A small statue of an angel made it more like a shrine. A wooden gazebo over a bamboo deck acted as a small place to worship or meditate. There was a gurgle as water bubbled in front of the angel.

I placed the cushion on the deck, dropped my robe and fell into a relaxed lotus position. Being a large yard with few nosey neighbors made it an ideal space for what I needed to do.

As I settled my mind, a slight noise interrupted my regimen. Jojo had come out to join me. I thought she would have rather slept, but her company would be welcome.

Dropping her robe, she settled down upon her cushion facing me. Our bare legs just brushed. Hands, palm upward, arms resting upon knees. Small shocks each time our fingers would touch.

We began a series of deep breathing. A system to get the mind quiet, the soul calmed and the spirit to have free reign of travel. I looked across and saw the contented smile upon her face. The little crinkle of lines at the upturned lips. The splash of freckles across her nose. With her eyes closed, she reminded me of the statue of the angel.

My mind calmed.

Her eyes opened and I fell in love all over again. That sparkle caused my breath to falter. I looked deep as she stared straight ahead. Her lips still slightly upturned in a complacent smile.

"I sensed the love from your soul. The true being of your existence. I traveled down through your mind, back to the beginning of this lifetime.

We met before we met. We met the real us all those years before. All those letters sent to each other. Even if I don't remember the exact words, I remember the feel. You wrote, not as a young girl, not as a cheerleader or gymnast, or whatever façade you were weaving. But you wrote with the soul of the poet, the nature lover, the adventuress, a child of the Earth.

I didn't feel hairstyle, eye color or figure. I felt the mind, the spirit, the potential and the love in those letters.

Just as you received the feel from a man who had things to say, deeds to do and a spirit he loved.

I had ideals and dreams yet unfulfilled. But with no one who would take the time to listen to me; no one to care to ask or wonder; no one except you.

It hurt to walk away, to leave you to follow your own trail and to be upon my own. You've suffered over those years. I feel that as we sit here in deep communion.

It hurts a little that I couldn't be there to help, to soften the blows, to ease your pains. But then you might not be the 'amazing you' that you've become."

We've been singing words of comfort and knowledge to others all through our lives, with little in return. We did it because it was expected, part of the design of our very existence.

Now, it is time to start singing songs to, for and with each other.

Point and counterpoint.

The Yin and Yang that has been the center of religions and ideologies for millennium.

Our song!

We have the melody in our souls, light and lilting, hauntingly soothing. Something to dance to if we want or just stand and hold each other as it washes over and cleanses our spirits. We know the words, but they are seldom spoken. They go from heart to heart, mind to mind, soul to soul.

I drift here, your consciousness brushes mine. Our spirits draw from one another and fulfill each other's needs. The purple light permeates our very presence and heals us with the sense of love and understanding.

I feel the bubble in my chest. The love wells up. But it is not that. Love is not the right word. It is stronger, more intense.

It is the feeling of completeness in each other. A sense that if you cease to exist, I will have never lived. The tendrils of feeling reach out from me to you, intermingling.

We are together, as one.

Our spirits soar through time and space."

We feel the tears of joy and contentment rain down upon us. I open my eyes to hear the thunder roll through our souls.

Your hand's in mine. A deep smile upon your lips. The purple glow surrounds us. We gently settle back down upon our cushions from the heights we have climbed both spiritually and physically."

Your hair was limp as the rain washed over us. We grabbed our cushions and with no care for clothing, we dashed, hand in hand for the back porch, laughing and happy in our newly discovered awareness.

CHAPTER 33

The night of the full moon was clear and warm. Our friends had begun to arrive. First George and his wife, Marion. He suggested we hold the service in the back yard. No close neighbors meant no interruptions.

It was a great idea.

He helped move the altar from the basement and Jojo began arranging the items upon it. With the White Goddess candle on the left, and the cup and saucer both positioned properly, along with the Athame and the common knife on the right, all in preparation for the evening rites.

Next, John and his lovely wife, Cynthia arrived.

Jojo began to fret; she and Paul rarely had people over.

"Nothing to worry about, Dear," I reassured her. "Give me a couple of minutes to make a list and you and the ladies can go shopping. I will begin to get dinner ready for all of us."

While I prepared a pot of tomato sauce, Jojo and the others left. It would be like days of old. Judy and I entertaining family and friends who dropped by unexpectedly. Large parties of people coming together to eat and socialize. Pounds of fresh pasta, breads, salads, and we would eat and enjoy a good time.

George saw the tears in my eyes, sensing my sorrow with his empathic spirit, he embraced me.

Embarrassed, I blamed the onions.

"Sure," he joked, "And I have a tepee for sale in Brooklyn."

The phone rang. With my hands busy, John answered; it was Joseph. They were bringing a couple they would instruct.

I said, sure, if they get here early enough they would be welcome for dinner, also.

He thought it a wonderful idea. Within the hour, the shoppers had returned, the pasta was cooked and the garlic bread browned to perfection.

Joseph and Kyra walked in with Bob and Annie Adams. They decided to explore and learn more of Wicca after all they had experienced.

We cobbled a makeshift table to accommodate all and enjoyed a simple dinner.

The sharing was the banquet.

Kyra came out in the yard as I ignited the kindling in the fire pit. She thought to incorporate it in the Circle. We moved the altar and arranged it all to her liking, since she would officiate the Rite.

A fire is always a relaxing feature.

At just before ten pm, with the full moon at its apogee, Kyra called us together.

"We have assembled this night to pay respects to the Moon and the Goddess. We will also help a haggard Spirit move onwards through the unfolding."

She looked each of us in the eye. "We have new practitioners tonight. Welcome to them and to all to this service."

The fire light reflected a somber and severe look on her face, setting an unusual and peculiar scene.

"WELCOME TO ALL GOOD AND GENTLE SPIRITS! COME JOIN US AT THE FIRE."

So began the service.

She raised the Athame and walked around our group to define the circle.

"With this Sacred Blade, I cast thee, the Circle of my Craft. May it be a doorway to more sacred circles beyond time and space. Let all who honor here be blessed, and all wickedness be deterred."

At this, small noises emanated from the altar. The black stone from the basement seemed to pulsate. Kyra ignored the distraction, raised the bell, and in the name of the Goddess, she cast the circle.

Turning back to the altar, lighting the white candle; with her arms wide and head tilted towards the sky, she intoned;

"GODDESS OF THE MOON,
OF NIGHT SKY YOU ARE QUEEN.
KEEPER OF WOMEN'S MYSTERIES
AND ALL THAT HAS BEEN,
MISTRESS OF THE TIDES,
EVER CHANGING, EBB, AND NEAP.
FILL US WITH YOUR WISDOM
AND KNOWLEDGE DEEP.
I BEG OF THEE TO SHIELD
AND GUIDE US WITH YOUR CHARMS
AND HOLD US, YOUR PRACTIONERS,
SAFELY IN YOUR LOVING ARMS."

She then went on to consecrate the Water and purify the Knife. And the rite continued until all had been satisfied, nearly.

As that ceremony ended, she asked Jojo to stand at the altar.

Kyra continued, "I have placed the entity, now known as Lian back as the crystal. She changed with the knowledge of what may befall her; is resigned to her fate. We will try to give her a better end."

"Sister Joanna, please take the Athame in your right hand."

Jojo reached down, grasped the knife firmly and raised it to eye level, point up, as if in offering to the Goddess. The firelight reflected weirdly upon it, casting strange shadows.

"Now, Sister, please take the crystal and hold that up in your left hand. That is what is Lian and the Magician."

She did as requested. We felt a disturbance in the tranquility of the Circle. We knew the Magician did not share this resignation of fates.

And Kyra began a strange and heretofore little known rite of ages past: 'The parting of the spirits'.

"Beloved Goddess, Power over all things, grant us thy divine Energy to divide these two spirits; allow the injured, healing; the wronged, righting; the anguished, peace. With 'The Magicians' own words, we justly gift him his reward; the Athame, this consecrated knife to send him in his rightful place ..."

"... HELL!"

She stopped and took a breath, removed the crystal from Jojo's hand and placed it onto the altar, in the consecrated dish and water.

We heard it sizzle and crackle.

"Joanna, dear daughter of the Goddess; of your own free will, will you allow these poor spirits to go each to their own rewards?"

"Yes Mother, may they each receive what they each knowingly asked for," she answered as if in a trance.

"Then, with the tip of the knife, pierce the stone," Kyra instructed.

I looked expectantly upon the altar, startled; a knife to push into rock?

"Spirit of the Goddess, accept our thanks, that, what we attempt here is proper and to Your liking," Kyra intoned.

Jojo placed the tip against the crystal, pushed with steady pressure.

And it slowly slid its way through the piece of solid stone. We felt the energy change in the Circle, both elation and fear, a slight wail of anguish. Lian had hope, anticipation, no matter what the outcome, she would be free; if she be condemned to the pits of hell, she would still be free of the curse and suffer gladly for it.

The Magician just plain raged. The wail continued, as if from the very depths of hades, itself. The crystal produced a small pinpoint of light, tickled on our scalps as it circled, darting hither and yon.

The stone, now not so lustrous, sat upon the altar, pulsating rapidly in great duress; feelings of hatred emanated, trying to beat pain into our senses. The knife tip, help fast in the stone as if it a sheath.

Annie looked at the light and questioned, "Why does it not move on? That is the Entity, that is Lian, isn't it?"

Kyra answered, "She is confused and lost."

Jojo questioned, "Then this crystal is just the Magician?"

"Yes, daughter of the Goddess; do what ye will."

Jojo raised the knife, the stone at eye level. It pulsated in rage. She looked deep, spat upon it and slammed the knife down onto the altar, back into the consecrated water; cursing,

"MAGICIAN, ROT – IN – HELL."

The stone hit the water and exploded; a ball of fire engulfed the altar. I dove for Jojo, dragging her backwards, to safety. Others screamed, throwing up their arms for protection. She was scared, but unharmed; a small smile of satisfaction across her lips.

As things calmed, and vision returned, Joseph was the first to comment about the light, "Some things are not simple," he began to explain in a slow, deep voice. "At times, even though not of their choosing, punishments are to be paid; forgiveness's given before the page can be turned."

"Well, that sucks," Annie replied. "Why doesn't someone help her," she asked, Motherly instincts taking over.

"With all the suffering this poor little spirit went through, someone must feel she has atoned for her sins," I exclaimed. "The sums on the page have been totaled; equaled, and the page is ready to be turned."

The energy in the Circle changed rapidly again. We calmed. We felt the quiet, the serenity; it surrounded us as a gentle sigh. With no discernible breeze, the candles flickered, the fire brightened and a lone, small leaf wafted in and amongst our little band. Tiny laughter filtered down to us.

Bob was the first to see and feel it. He took his wife's hand, pointed and whispered, "Abby," as his eyes glistened.

That leaf danced in the face of her earthly Mother, encircled hers', then Bob's head. We watched as both parents cried, while Abby pirouetted in front of their tears, fluttering as if to dry them.

We felt the spirit, the happiness, and forgiveness she emanated. We watched as Abby drifted to Lian. We heard the titters, felt the glee. Dancing around each other, two little girls game played as they might have done in life. The love, happiness and the forgiveness of those little spirits imbued those same feelings into our souls.

And - as if their game over, it was time to run home, hand in hand laughing the entire way. They encircled and danced around us all. Freely giving and sharing the love and happiness their spirits held, filling our hearts. An extra moment or two in front of Annie and Bob, the two little entities danced their way upwards to the waiting heavens.

"MOTE IT BE," Kyra whispered.

We stood, each alone and together, quietly holding hands, weeping, smiling, sharing; knowing we witnessed a True Miracle.

CHAPTER 34

The circle opened; the altar artifacts removed to the basement. Our friends began to take their leave.

John and his wife, Cynthia came to bid us goodnight, thanking us for a wonderful, exciting evening. Their experiences would be the subject of stories for some time throughout the covens.

Bob and Annie also headed out. The two couples were going to the diner for more coffee, and a bit quieter conversation. Being police officers, they needed to talk about what they could do to close his daughters' case, and in brighter, less mysterious surroundings.

George and Marion also needed to leave. The lateness of the hour found them in a hurry, as their dog would need relief. They planned a service, two weeks hence; a new moon ceremony and we were invited.

Jojo accepted for us.

I stopped her, telling George we would let them know. She turned, giving me a strange look and a little squeak.

They went to say goodnight to the others.

She rounded on me, "What do you mean by not giving them a definite answer," she whispered. "These people are friends, helped us through a difficult time and you say 'we will see'?"

"Jojo, I don't know if I will be here in two weeks," I informed her.

She gave me a hard and steely look.

"Just what do you mean by that," she hissed.

"I have a house, a family on the East Coast," I reminded her. "I need to get back there, get things done, bills paid. I am sure I have a pile of mail that I need to go through."

"So, you are leaving me, just like that," she questioned angrily, "Running out?"

"Now wait a minute," I began, "I just buried my wife. I have duties to attend to."

Her eyes glowed bright, as two lit coals trying to burn through my skull.

"What about me," she threw back in a raspy voice.

"You have those same duties here," I answered.

"Soon you will find those items in drawers and closets needing to be packed up and given to family and friends. The weights in the basement might be good for Johnny."

She looked at me, puzzled'

"The Altar boy," I reminded her.

I took her hand. "I have the same thing I need to be doing at my house. I think we need to do some of these things alone. Some parts of mourning need to be done in private."

Tears misted her eyes. I guess it was catchy, but she nodded. Her emotions had been running high; having gone through so very much in such a short period. She felt abandoned again and it carried away her good sense, for a minute, anyway.

Seeing her smile, I knew she understood.

Joseph had walked George and Marion out to their car. He now returned with a stranger, a younger woman. They had a conversation before walking over to us.

"Frank, Joanna, let me introduce Samantha Campbell. She is the niece of my friend Henry."

I turned to him with a lost look.

"Henry who left us the geode," he went on to explain.

Samantha picked up the conversation, "I don't know exactly what happened to Uncle Henry," she shared. "The last I had heard, he was living in his cabin on the mountain."

"Now I can't find him. I found paperwork showing that Joseph was his friend. I came here seeking help. No one knows anything about his passing, or where he was buried, or even who buried him. I don't even know who sent the information out that he had died."

"He told me several times that I was in the will as his sole surviving relation, but no one notified me about the reading of the will. Now I learn the property is up for sale and the real estate knows only a lawyers name."

She was under great duress. Kyra made the girl comfortable at the kitchen table.

While we retrieved refreshments, Jojo let out a small yelp and reached to her throat.

MERLIN pulsated.

We looked at each other, I whispered, "I guess that means we should help Samantha, so I won't be long gone from here."

Jojo glanced at me with relief and a smile.

We walked back to the table, the refreshments on the tray, to find what kind of trouble this dead Wizard had in store for us ...

EPILOGUE

I had been home on the east coast for several days, clearing out Judy's things. I gave away clothes to Good Will, the kids split up some of her favorite knick-knacks in remembrance. The rest I will hold for now. When Jojo next visits, she can decide what she wants to keep or give away. She had helped Judy in the hunt for most of them.

It had been a few lonely days, with scant communication between us, being busy to rush through this process.

I sat doing what I did best.

It was just a quick e-mail; a reminder that I was thinking of her.

Jojo,
As a writer, my dreams are sometimes real. I awoke with this on my mind.

> *It will be so pleasant*
> *With you, hand in hand*
> *To wander through the meadows*
> *In sunshine so grand.*
> *I stoop to pluck a flower*
> *To place behind your ear…*
> *Then I awoke to find*
> *That you're not really here.*

I will love the times we sit
To enjoy the evening breezes.
We'll watch the firefly dance
As happily as it pleases.
To reach to find your hand
Awaiting eagerly to grasp mine.
But then morning breaks and
You're nowhere; But on my mind.
And how perfect will it be
To hold you close and ... (sigh)
Feel your cheek on mine;
No more reasons to cry.
Knowing that our spirits
Did finally find the way.
Then I awoke,
  Alone,
    Again
      Today.

It's time for sleep,
Perchance to dream
Of course I'll dream of you.
But we're apart and feeling Sad
So, this will have to do...
Late tonight, if on your arm
You feel a slight insistent tug;
It's only me, sleep walking through
Just looking for a hug.

Me!

A preview of the next,
"A WITCH, IN TIME, AGAIN…

THE MEETING

Five men representing a goodly portion of the wealth and power in the world filed into the conference room.

They had arrived in private jets and were chauffeured up the mountain in their limousines.

The room was a nominal size, comfortably apportioned. Rich cherry wood and mahogany finished off with rosewood inlays surrounded them. The house, itself was large, but not huge. It was set back, tucked in a niche on a mountain. The winding road was all the security needed as it was lined with gadgets that afforded absolute privacy.

Nodding in reverence to the white-haired gentleman who sat at the head of the table in front of the picture window, they stood, waiting.

The light glared through the glass, distorting his features, making him unrecognizable to those in attendance.

After another moment of silence, he motioned for them to sit.

There was no chatter, no greetings.

No refreshments but water.

One man stood, "the first phase is complete, Sir. In the ten years the fertilizers and the other compounds take to leech through the soil, they will continue to deliver the toxins."

226

The old man waved his hand, as if flicking at a gnat.

Another man stood. "The mechanism works excellent. Virtually all the energy anomalies are accounted for, worldwide. We have one with a slight deterrence. We are working it out."

A third man stood, "The new self-pollinating plants are ready. We need the final ingredient and we can begin the live testing."

As he sat, the fourth man stood, hesitant, "Sir, Gregory Rogers is beyond our scope. The official report shows him dying during a failed break in of a residence. He supposedly was shot and killed by the local police."

"The story from the actual, private account of the chief of police is that he died in an attack, being subsumed by an evil entity."

The last man stood. A pause as he wet his lips. "The front is ready sir. We will no longer need him once the statutes are in place. But that is your call, afterwards. We will need another Warlock for the spells. Magicks is the only way he wins. Other avenues to his victory are closed to us. Any different aspect to his success cannot be in place in time for the election."

The old man nodded, and with the wave of his hand dismissed all that wealth.

He sat quietly as the room emptied.

Turning his chair to look out through the one way, blast-proof window overlooking the valley in the Alps; he finally smiled.